DOWN

TO

RiDE

A NOVEL

JAKAYLA GABRIELLE

To those of you who think you should have it all figured out by...Give yourself some time to grow and enjoy the ride.

DOWN
TO
RIDE

CHAPTER 1

SIOBHAN

Four more hours.

I had four long, boring hours to go 'til I was back home, in front of the new big screen tv Mama had just bought us. *The Wayans' Brothers* was coming on at 7:30 and Mama knew nothing came between me and Marlon. Marlon was the goofy younger brother of the famous Wayans siblings and he was all mine, at least he was in my head. All the other girls I knew loved Shawn, and for good reason too. But I always had my eye on Marlon. I dreamt about the day we would meet, get married, and run off into the sunset together, like the people in the movies.

Instead of being at home watching reruns until the new episode came on, I was out with Mama, shopping for school clothes.

She made such a big deal about senior year 'til I just really didn't care anymore. I knew I wasn't going to college, at least not right out of high school. But Mama didn't know that yet. She just knew I had a plan and I did a good job of making her think that. Anytime she would burst into my bedroom, I pretended to be studying. Most of the time, I was playing M.A.S.H and forging my results so that they would reflect a life that included Marlon as my husband, a few goofy Wayans babies and I would be a stay-at-home mom who pushed a Bentley everywhere I went. A girl could dream, couldn't she?

"Siobhan, I know you hear me. Come out and let me see. I don't have all day," Mama fussed.

For the first time in 17 years, Mama was rushing me out of the store. She didn't have to tell me twice though. I threw on the few outfits she tossed in the basket and smiled liked everything was fine. But things were far from fine. I just wanted to get out of that store. Nothing EVER fit my body right. Everything was always too long, too short, or too tight. I could never find cute shoes that fit, and it seemed like fashion designers refused to believe or accept that tall, voluptuous Black girls exist. Well, I do, and I hated shopping for this reason alone. The fact that Mama always picked out some granny outfits and windbreakers for every day of the week made it 100 times worse. Then, she would get herself the matching sets, like we were twins or something.

"Siobhan, come on! I have somewhere to be!" Mama fussed again.

"I'm coming! These jeans won't go all the way up!" I whined.

"Let me see."

I stumbled out of the dressing room, barely able to move or breathe. Mama fell out laughing. "I'm glad you find this hilarious," I said. She waved her hand, sending me back, still laughing. "Mama, I'm almost 18. Let me pick my clothes."

One thing about Shanté Butler, she was counting down the days until I turned 18, so my reminder was never necessary. In my family, parents put their kids out as soon as they graduated high school, if they even graduated. That was a big *if* too.

Where we lived, in Los Angeles, everybody's parents had a little money. But turning 18 was a big deal for the kids I grew up with. They were different from my cousins. They had dreams, and parents who could help make them come true. The thing I was looking forward to the most was moving out and getting to choose my favorite cereal at the grocery store. I also couldn't wait to come in and out of my front door whenever I wanted. Nobody was about to put me outside in the summer until the streetlights came on. I could do whatever I wanted.

"Forty-three dollars and sixty-five cents," the cashier said, as she smacked on a piece of bubble gum, waiting for Mama to write a check.

Mama handed the cashier her check and took a deep breath as she ran it. She finally exhaled when the girl passed her the receipt. She wasn't laughing anymore...More like relieved. We were heading toward the exit when the alarm went off. A man in a faded, striped button-down shirt ran over and snatched our bags from us, emptying them all over the counter, cross-referencing Mama's receipt with every item. Everything checked out, but the lady checking us out had forgotten to remove a security tag. Everyone in the store was standing around watching us. The man removed the tag and walked away without uttering a single word.

As I stuffed our clothes back in the bags, I looked over at Mama who was pretending to soothe my three-year-old baby brother, Chase, but I could see her hands shaking. "Let's go," she said, eyeing the cashier, who rolled her eyes and moved on to the next customer. I looked back at the lady, then at Mama, who was already halfway to the car. "We're stopping by the Goodwill on the way home. I need to see what kinds of purses them old ladies threw away this week," she said, laughing, but still clearly shaken up.

When we pulled up to the Goodwill, Mama looked over her checkbook and counted her cash while I unbuckled Chase. "Damn," she said, hitting the steering wheel. I knew that meant she had overspent, and something was either getting returned or we would be eating pork and beans and rice, or SPAM for a few nights, until she got paid again.

"Mama, you can take some of my clothes back. It's not a big deal. I still have clothes from the summer to wear."

She couldn't look at me with a straight face to match her reply. "It's okay. We just gon' have to tough it out 'til Tuesday. You need new clothes for school."

I pulled a wad of cash from my pocket and counted out four dollars and handed it to her. "Let's go get you a purse. Hopefully, we find one with some money in it like last time," I joked, hoping she'd smile and show off that one deep dimple I loved so much. It worked. I browsed the shoe section to see if anybody had donated some Fila's I could clean up. The only pair left was snatched up by some chick with a dirty pair of flip flops on. Her feet looked like she had been Bedrockin' it everywhere.

My only option for shoes was a pair of dingy, white church shoes with barely a heel. I gave up and met Mama and Chase at the checkout line. We were next in line when Mama looked like she'd seen a ghost. I waved my hand in front of her face and she didn't even blink. "Mama!" I said loudly. "Go!"

The cashier was growing impatient. She was just as rude as the cashier from the last store. Mama started stuttering and fumbling around in her purse. After a few seconds, I just paid for everything, grabbed the bag and headed for the door. She lingered behind me. Then, some Mexican woman and a girl about my age walked by. The woman stopped abruptly, causing the girl to run into the back of her feet. She screamed as she bit her bottom lip and massaged her heel. When she turned back around, she had a weird look on her face, looking right at us.

I turned to notice Mama staring right back in the woman's direction. It was like they were trying to see who was going to speak first. "Daya, it's nice to see you again. It's been a long time," Mama said. The woman rolled her eyes before sucking her teeth and walking off. Mama ran up to her and grabbed her arm. The lady whipped around and pushed Mama so hard that she fell into the side of their cart and the manager came running to the front of the store. Mama straightened her clothes as everyone in the store stopped what they were doing to see what was going on. On the way to the car, I kept looking over my shoulder and caught the woman watching as we walked away. Her nasty scowl dissolved when Mama climbed in the front seat.

As we pulled away, I started drilling Mama. "Who was that? And why did she put her hands on you?" She still hadn't answered me by the time we made it home, but I knew that wasn't the end of that situation. Shanté Butler was no punk, and it was unlike her to just walk away from someone putting their hands on her. But she did and she was quiet for the rest of the day. I had never seen her so zoned out before. Everything she said and did after that felt foreign to me. Mama had gotten soft on me.

CHAPTER 2

CARMEN

After shopping for school clothes, Mami stopped by my favorite taco spot for lunch and got me a big ole burrito, with all the fixings. I couldn't wait to get home and stuff my face while dancing the meringue and tearing through my new threads. Nothing made me happier than getting new clothes that needed work. I mean, where was the fun in wearing clothes that everybody else was rocking?

As soon as we made it home, I ran to my room. I turned my boombox on, emptied my bag onto my bed, took a big bite of my food, and went to work.

It took for Mami to come to my room for dinner before I realized the sun had set. "Baby, I need to talk to you," she said. I pushed over the pile of clothes near me and turned my sewing machine off. She sat on the corner of my bed, twiddling her thumbs, clearly avoiding what was really on her mind. I cleared my throat after a few minutes of her peeking over my shoulder.

"I know things have been tight around here. Things at the cleaners aren't picking up and I need some help. I know you're saving for school and all…so I wanted to know if it would be okay for Elisio to move in with us?"

Elisio was Mami's lazy, broke-ass boyfriend. He never did anything but start trouble whenever he came around. Her thinking he should move in was bigger than us needing help with our bills, so I respectfully replied, "Mami, you're the adult. Do whatever you think is best." She sighed heavily, kissed my cheek, and picked up one of the shirts I had been working on.

"Mami, who was that at the store today?" I asked. I knew Mami, and she didn't just go around pushing people. She had a loud mouth, but that was about as far as anything ever went with her and anybody, other than Elisio's ass. He couldn't keep his hands to himself most of the time, so she made it a point to show him she wasn't to be played with.

9

She pretended to be checking herself out in my mirror as I waited for an answer.

"What? Who was who?" she responded.

"That woman you pushed. Did you know her?"

"Carmen, I'm having a good day, okay? Elisio's taking me salsa dancing, and I want to have a good time. No negativity, okay?"

She kept stretching my shirt over her breasts, down to her hips, turning to the side to get a better look at her booty.

"Mind if I wear this on my date tonight?" she asked. Without waiting for an answer, she pranced out of the room, with my shirt squeezing her love handles.

When the coast was clear, I pulled a shoebox from the top of my closet. I was always careful not to pull it out while anybody, especially Mami, was in my room. She knew I had been saving up for college, but she didn't know how much I had, and that's the way I liked things. The less she knew, the better. My last count was at about $2,485. It wasn't a lot, but it was a start. I figured I could find a way to pick up some more of Mami's customers from the dry cleaners she worked at. The prices for alterations had gotten too high and her boss, Mr. Manny, started losing business, which caused him to cut Mami's hours more and more each week.

When the customers started to complain, Mami offered to do their alterations for them, but she passed the buck to me because she couldn't get from under Elisio long enough to even remember what day it was. My customers paid me decently, but it still wasn't enough for me to be able to move to attend NYU. I barely had enough for room and board, but I had seen my fair share of eviction notices and I knew things weren't going to change around there any time soon.

As I grabbed a few twenties and put my shoebox back in the closet, Mami came back in my room asking me to help her stretch *my* shirt. Her stomach was hanging out, and her jeans were way too tight, but Mami didn't listen to anybody. Sure, she'd ask for your opinion, but that didn't mean she was going to listen. "You look fine Mami. Now, go!" I said, pushing her out of my room.

"I left a plate of Arroz con Pollo in the microwave," she shouted from the living room as Elisio laid on his car horn outside.

She cursed him out on her way to the car. Anybody within 10 miles of our apartment could hear them every time they argued. I enjoyed any time I got to myself because things were always hectic with them both around. It was as if they couldn't function without fighting and making up. Mami was always nice afterward, but it never lasted long.

Later, I ate dinner in peace in my room and went back to sewing, while my favorite Tejano, Selena, helped me quiet the voices in my head. She was the inspiration behind so many of my designs. I used to dream of growing up and dressing her for her shows. But after her passing, I decided to honor her memory by putting my little Colombian heart into all of my designs. My first finished piece was bustier, like the ones she used to wear during her performances. I kept it on a mannequin near my bed, as inspiration…so I would never forget why I started.

CHAPTER 3

SIOBHAN

The first day of school was a few days away and everything that I thought was cute in the store looked like crap in my closet, and the floor of my bedroom was covered in clothes. To make matters worse, I heard one of Mama's clients pulling up outside, coming to get her hair done. I knew it was Ms. Sharonda because she always argued with her boyfriend when he would drop her off, in *her* car.

I wish Mama worked in a shop because almost every one of them was loud and ghetto…Always coming over ruining my mood and talking over the tv. Mama always made me cater to them so she could get them in and out with no breaks.

I could hear Mama coming down the hallway singing the alphabet song with Chase as soon as the front door closed. He always skipped right over everything between G and Q. He was too adorable to be corrected, so we went along with it. "Siobhan, can you please put Chase down for a nap? I need to press Sharonda's hair." Chase started throwing a fit when she passed him to me. Snot, tears, and slob were all over his little, red face. As soon as Mama closed the door, he calmed down and sat in the middle of my pile of clothes. I turned the tv to Nickelodeon and kept sorting through my outfits, randomly asking Chase for his little opinion anytime I couldn't decide between two tops.

"I'm hungry. How about you?" I asked, not expecting him to respond. But somehow, he always understood anything I said that involved.

With Chase on my hip, I headed to the kitchen to find us something to snack on. Mama and Ms. Sharonda were gossiping, as usual, when we walked in. They got quiet as if I hadn't already gotten an earful of them talking about Daddy.

Mama always complained about how all he ever did for me was pay child support. But Ms. Sharonda was always complaining because she couldn't even get that much from her kids' daddies. They would go back and forth, comparing their men problems, like there was nothing else going on in the world.

"Siobhan, girl, every time I see you, that baby is on your hip. Won't be long before you have your own, huh?" Ms. Sharonda joked.

Mama didn't look up nor comment. Then, I heard, "Shit! Girl, you burned me!" Ms. Sharonda hissed at Mama. Mama looked at me and smiled. I grabbed some peanut butter and Saltine crackers for Chase and myself and we headed back to my room.

It was just my luck that Chase would be dead asleep when *The Wayans Bros.* came on. By that time, Mama was finishing some dookie braids on another client, Ms. Dionne, and I knew she was about to interrupt my show to have me do something else. Happened every single time. I waited about 30 minutes after Ms. Dionne left, and still no Mama. Then, the smell of pork chops frying on the stove circulated through the vents. Mama finally knocked on my door and stuck her head in. "Dinner will be ready in a few. Come make some Kool-Aid," she said.

That night we had the most awkward family dinner. We always sat across from one another, while Chase played over his food in his highchair, but I could tell something was on her mind. Fried pork chops with rice & gravy was our favorite meal and she was picking over hers. Finally, she laid her fork in her plate and watched me until I felt her eyes burning a hole through my skull. I kept eating, and with a mouth full of food, asked, "What?" She looked concerned, as she watched Chase smash his rice. I finished chewing and sat my fork down to give her my undivided attention.

"You graduate this year. Remind me of this plan of yours, again," she said.

I knew this was coming. My counselor at school bugged me about having a plan for after high school for most of junior year. Truth be told, I didn't know what I liked or what I wanted to do. I bet it would be cool to work in television, but Mama made it clear that no daughter of hers would be caught dead shaking their tail in a rapper's music video. I tried to explain that there was more to tv than music videos, and I wish Marlon had responded to my letter so I could've proven it to her.

"Things are about to start changing around here," she continued.

I started back eating, but this time it was me picking over my food. Chase fell asleep in his chair, so I jumped at the opportunity to go clean him up and put him to bed. Once I finished cleaning the kitchen, Mama came and sat on the corner of my bed. She was still trying to talk to me about my future, but I wasn't trying to hear it.

"Where are you going to school? You been looking for a job? I'm serious. I'm not taking care of you forever," she said.

I played dumb long enough for her to get frustrated, and she finally backed down and left. As soon as I heard Anita Baker, I knew she was getting in bed and that would be the last I'd hear from her that night, so I pulled my picture of Marlon from under my pillow, held it close to my heart, and fell asleep.

CHAPTER 4

CARMEN

The first day of my senior year at Beachwood High was bittersweet. I was happy to be graduating, but I hated it there. That school was full of crackheads, dope dealers, hoochies and teachers that just didn't give a damn about us. I always had the best grades in my classes because I was like the only one who did the work. I mean, the guidance counselor and I were on a first-name basis. She even had me over for dinner to help me research colleges before. I stopped going when she said, "There's no future in being a fashion designer, for someone like you. Be more sensible with your career goals".

No matter how nervous I was, Mami always knew

how to make me feel better. She turned my favorite song up.
Como la Flor rocked the walls of our tiny, rundown apartment
as Mami and I danced together like we used to when I was
little. When we were moving around between homeless
shelters, Mami had a small boombox that she took
everywhere we went. She said good music could help you
forget all your problems. That statement had never been truer
than at that very moment. She spun me around and I fell into
her arms as Elisio burst into my room, wiping sleep from his
eyes.

"Apaga esa mierda!" he shouted.

"We speak English around here, asshole," I said.

"Ouch, Mami! What was that for?" I asked, rubbing
my arm. She was always pinching me like I was a little kid.
Then, as usual, she pushed Elisio back out into the hallway,
coddling him like a baby.

I had finished getting dressed and was leaving for
the bus stop when she caught me at the front door.

"They're gonna shut the lights off if we… if I don't
pay on it today." I ran back to my room, grabbed $50 from
my stash, and handed it over. "I'll have it back to you by
Friday, mija. I promise," she lied. She grabbed my chin and
smeared her lipstick all over me until I pulled away and ran
down the stairs. Just before I closed the front door, I heard

her shout, "Enchiladas for dinner! Don't be late. Oh, and tell André hi for me".

As soon as I got to the school parking lot, a fight broke out. What was the first day of school if nobody fought, right? Something told me that it was Jasmine and Vanessa still fighting over Marcus's dusty ass, and I was right. But I had other problems to deal with, so while teachers broke up the fight, I ran to the restroom as fast as I could, hoping nobody would see me. Just before I got to the door, it happened.

"Yo Carmen, what's up, baby? Why you been ignoring my calls? Your mom told me you was at home. We good? You look good...like really good," André said, licking his big crusty lips.

He snatched my arm and pulled me in for a hug and I smacked the shit out of him. "Yo, what the hell was that for?" he asked, falling into a locker, holding his jaw. As a crowd began to form, I disappeared inside of the restroom. The smell of fresh paint made my head throb as I leaned against the sink, going over my class schedule. After waiting him out for a few minutes, I ran to the cafeteria to grab a bite to eat before the first bell. André was posted up at a table with a few guys when I came out of the line stuffing my mouth.

When the bell rang, I started walking toward homeroom and felt someone pull on my backpack. Terry, one of André's boys, handed me a letter that was covered in food stains and smeared blue ink. I was to balling it up when I looked up and saw André standing in the doorway, two classrooms down, watching me. I made it a point to look right into his eyes, open it all the way up, then I ripped it up and threw it down in the middle of the hallway. Terry went behind me and picked up every piece and gave it to André. I watched as he stuck it in his pocket and went inside, scowling and nodding his head at me.

"Ms. Martinez, close the door and find your seat," Mr. Sutton said.

All eyes were on me as I slouched down in my desk and threw my hood, then laid my head on my desk. It was going to take a prayer and a miracle to get through the school year, and I was running low on faith that either of the two would ever be enough.

CHAPTER 5

SIOBHAN

The senior wing of Pulliam Preparatory Academy was live on the first day back. The class of 2000 was running through the hallways like a bunch of lunatics, making fools of themselves spraying silly string and banging on lockers. Principal Hawkins let them be. She stood to the side and laughed at their antics until they went too far.

I was standing at my locker, hanging up pictures of Me, Chase, Mama and Daddy when I caught a whiff of the most breathtaking scent. I turned around and there was this guy I had never seen before trying to get into his locker, while everyone stood around and watched. The guys gossiped like girls while the girls stared, twirling the ends of their hair winking and blowing kisses at him.

He had a nicely trimmed goatee lining his sun-kissed skin, and his clothes were fresh, like they had just come off of an ironing board. The creases in his jeans were about so stiff that I just knew they'd stand up on their own when he took 'em off.

When it became too painful to watch him continue to struggle, I went over, took the piece of paper from his hands, and opened his locker. He flashed a half smile, just enough for me to see he had a beautiful set of teeth. I smiled back and ducked inside of homeroom just seconds before the tardy bell rang.

Somehow, I got stuck in homeroom with every single one of my classmates that had made the last two years complete hell for me. From talking about my black gums and skin to my big thighs, I had heard it all from them. I would have thought that with our school being one big melting pot, that most of them would have been used to brown skin by then.

While everyone chatted amongst themselves, talking over the school announcements, I buried my head into a book, while simultaneously hoping no one noticed I was even there. Then, a deep and unusually smooth voice asked, "Is this seat taken?" A chill crept down my spine as I took a deep breath and lowered the book, looking right into the eyes of the new guy.

"I can sit somewhere else…but I'd rather be back here, hiding with you," he said.

He smiled bigger that time and two gold teeth exposed themselves. He had the most perfect smile. Straight, white, and beautiful complimented by the refreshing scent of Winterfresh gum. "No one's sitting here," I said.

"What's this?" he asked, looking around my book for the title.

I hadn't had much experience with talking to guys, and my mouth was as dry as the Sahara Desert. I couldn't form a single sentence, so I just smiled and laughed, again. Nothing was even funny.

"I'm Tremaine," he said, holding his hand out.

The last thing I wanted to do was shake his hand. The sweat seeping from my clammy palms was nothing compared to the sweat I was soaking up with the pits of my bright yellow blouse.

"I tried to tell my uncle that teenagers don't shake hands when they meet, but he never listens to me," Tremaine said.

I couldn't think of a single response that wouldn't make me sound like a complete idiot, so I smiled, again, and went back to reading. I kept checking him out from the corner of my eyes, as he pulled out his Walkman and put his head down.

Homeroom flew by and I couldn't wait to get out of there. I was halfway to first period when I realized that had I never even told him my name. I bolted to the restroom, hyperventilating like I had just met a celebrity. Then, in walked Brandy. For a moment in time, we were friends. Then, she found a new group of girls to hang with that rocked all the latest fashions and had boyfriends who practically worshipped them. She came to Pulliam Prep in 10th grade like me and made a name for herself, while I worked to remain invisible.

"Might as well not even waste your time crushing on him. He'll be mine by the end of the week," she said.

"Aren't you and Cody together? You can't have two boyfriends," I said.

"Says who?"

At first, Brandy came off as sweet, but over time she became as mean as a snake. It was like somebody flipped a switch one day and turned her into a full-blown bitch. I watched as she pulled her long, jet black curls into a bun similar to mine and readjusted the socks in her bra to look natural. She was about three shades lighter than me but coated her skin in a foundation that was almost three shades lighter than her. She walked around looking like she'd just been embalmed and thought people feared her because of her "strong" personality.

Most people at school thought she had it all. But I knew the truth. Her parents had fallen on hard times too many times to count and I watched as they fought with the people who came out to turn their utilities off every month. She lived a few houses down from me, but no one at school would ever know it, because she never let any of them come over. She led them to believe that she lived in the Hills and that she chose public school over private school so that her parents could afford to get her a brand-new BMW for her graduation gift. That lie still spoke volumes about who she really was, but our classmates were too dumb to notice.

By lunchtime, I had managed to calm my nerves and follow my usual routine of eating my lunch under the big oak tree in the schoolyard, alone. Before I could set my food up to eat, Tremaine was headed my way with a book tucked under his arm.

"Hope you don't mind if I join you," he said. "I stopped by the library and picked up a lil' something".

His large, manly hands nearly covered the title, but I was still able to make out from the cover that he had picked up *The Color Purple*. I tried to keep reading *Tuck Everlasting* like he wasn't even there, but I could feel his breath on my neck as I turned to catch him looking over my shoulder. "What's that about?" he asked. Finally, I closed my book and turned to face him.

"You've never heard of Tuck Everlasting?" I asked, laughing.

"I'm asking, ain't I?"

"It's about this family that can't die," I said, turning the page.

"Would you want to live forever?" he asked.

"Right now, I just want to finish this book."

He got up and walked off, leaving his book behind. I tried to catch up to him but as soon as I picked it up, a folded piece of paper fell out. It had a phone number and a message that said, "Call me if you need me". The phone number that followed was small and choppy like the ink was going out of the pen. I could've waited until I got home to call him, but after that stunt I had just pulled, I wouldn't want to talk to me either. One good thing came out of it though. I got the digits and I had a reason to talk to him again. I just had to find a way to apologize.

CHAPTER 6

CREMAINE

A year before I moved to Los Angeles, I was out on the block in my old hood in Shreveport, Louisiana. I was the man. I was gettin' paper and my granny wanted for nothing. It was funny how that worked out. She was supposed to be taking care of me after My ma died and my only brother, Travis, went to jail for killing her. A fight over a small bag of coke got her pushed off the front porch, where she hit her head on the last concrete step. Life ain't been the same since, man.

After moving to L.A. with my uncle, Tony, I came

real close to postin' up long enough to get a Greyhound ticket back home. He pulled my ass off the corner and beat me in front of my customers. Embarrassed me enough to where I never thought about stepping foot back on a street corner, 'til my first day of school. I was expected to spend my last year of high school in some fancy ass school where the girls ain't know nothin' about nothin'. All they thought about was how they looked and who they wanted next.

I had two strikes on me already and the last thing I needed was some lil' girl tryna trap me or catch me up. I had made it 18 years with no kids, and as long as Unc had anything to do with it, I wouldn't have none til' he was dead and gone.

I didn't even care about getting fly for the first day. I threw on one of my old pair of khakis, a white tee and some white Chucks. Unc never let me leave the house without cologne. He always said, "Son, it's one thing to look like a man, but you gotta smell like one too". I'd had my fair share of problems from thinking like a man and I ain't want no trouble, from him, or them folks at that school, so I let him think he knew better than me.

He dropped me off down the street so I could walk up alone. I ain't need nobody sweatin' me about pullin' up in a busted station wagon. Unc understood though. He said when he was my age, Granny didn't even have a car. He said they walked or caught the bus everywhere, if the neighbor wouldn't give 'em a ride. I was almost up to the front steps of the school when I heard his ride popping and squealing, passing the line of cars and other kids walking up. Everybody turned around and started laughing, so I kept it moving. I ain't play 'bout my family, but I also wasn't tryna go to jail in California.

I ain't know if it was my clothes, Unc's cologne or if everybody knew I was new, but heads turned and girls started smiling and whispering, everywhere I went. This girl named Brandy came rubbing up against me, like she had to touch me to get to her locker that was three feet away from mine. "Oops", she said, dropping her notebooks and turning all the way around, then bending over with her ass on display for the whole school to see.

"You good," I told her. I put my backpack up, grabbed my schedule, a notebook and pencil, and headed to homeroom.

It seemed like every seat was taken, except for the one at the back by this really pretty honey. For a minute, she didn't speak to me. But when the principal started goin' over the announcements, and the class got rowdy at the mention of the class of 2000, I saw her smile a lil' bit. When I saw her let her guard down after just barely getting her to let me sit down, I stuck my hand out and introduced myself.

She was really into this book and I ain't have nothing else to do, so I peeped over her shoulder so I could read it too. That shit was boring, and I could feel my eyes getting heavy, so I laid my head down, pretending to be listening to music to avoid more girls tryna holla at me.

I ain't know my way around yet, so I had to keep asking folks for directions. Everybody but the dudes helped me. Everything in me wanted to leave halfway through the day, but by fourth period, I noticed the girl with the book was in almost all my classes. Since everybody else was either tryna holla or tryna front on me, I went everywhere she did. Shit was cool 'til lunch and she started trippin'.

Normally, I would've popped off, but I felt like something was different with this girl. She was real pretty. I'm talkin' video girl pretty. I was gonna get to know her real soon, but first, I needed to figure out my angle. I ain't need Unc cock blocking so I had to figure this one out by myself.

CHAPTER 7

CARMEN

No sooner than when school started back up did my clientele pick up. I was working fast, stitching a hem in Ms. Gonzales's dress for work, to get her out of there and to give my ears a break from her non-stop talking.

"So, you excited about the wedding?" she asked.

"What wedding?"

"Your mom didn't tell you?"

"Tell me what?"

Then, she became very tight-lipped as I finished up. She paid me and was leaving when Mami came in. She could tell I was pissed because I didn't even acknowledge her. I just turned and went back to my room, slamming the door behind me. She followed me, as always, trying to smooth things over.

"What is your problem, mija? You have been very cranky lately," she said.

I started to look for my outfit for the next day, trying my hardest to fight back the tears and ignore her. When I couldn't take it anymore, I exploded.

"So, you're going to marry that bastard? When were you going to tell me?"

"Carmen, I don't need your permission to get married or to be with any man. I'm the adult. You're the child," she said, trying to remain calm.

"Am I a child? Or only when it's convenient for you? You can never seem to do anything for me anymore, but you have all the time in the world for him. I wish Papi was here. I hate it here!"

"Then, leave!" she shouted. "Get the hell out!"

I had never even met my father. I knew only the bits and pieces she decided to share with me, so after seeing how much it upset her to even tell me about him and their past, I decided that any time she wouldn't leave me alone, I knew exactly what to do. But this time she didn't just get up and leave. She walked over, stood right in my face, and slapped me so hard that my face burned for the rest of that night.

"Tu pequeña perra! I have struggled every day since you were born. I have done unspeakable things to make sure you've always had what you needed. But because I have fallen on hard times again and finally found real love, I'm not shit to you? You're right. I wish your no-good ass padre was here. God knows I need a break from your selfish, inconsiderate, disrespectful ass! You have no idea about the things I had to do to get into this country so that you could have a better chance at life! And this is how you repay me?"

She didn't give me a chance to respond, nor did I want to. I had heard it all before. She got like that any time she had no real defense for doing stupid stuff. I didn't have the smallest amount of sympathy for her because she put us in that situation.

The next day, I picked up a newspaper on my way to school. I spent my entire lunch circling and calling about job ads, even the ones I was too young or not qualified for. Almost every one I called about had been filled, but I wasn't ready to give up though. I was willing to check every newspaper, every day to find better paying work and save the money that I needed. I was determined to get myself from underneath Mami's thumb, one way or another.

CHAPTER 8

SIOBHAN

The next day, at school, I tried to steer clear of Tremaine. I hid at the back of the class again and watched as the minutes on the clocks of each of my classes ticked away.

After school, I came home to a note on the fridge that read, "Get Chase from Mama Joyce. I'll be late tonight." Mama Joyce served as the neighborhood daycare, for the Black kids. When we first moved in, I was about six years old. Mama said things were changing, and the people who lived within a few blocks of us said they didn't want us "taking over their neighborhood", so they stopped letting us in their daycares and tried to keep us out of their schools. Mama

Joyce had just retired from a job as a teacher and opened her home to low-income families in the area. She babysat me while Mama worked day and night cleaning houses and office buildings in The Hills.

I walked in the door and immediately got fussed at. Mama Joyce never locked her front door during business hours. Everyone knew not to mess with her and *her* babies. "Shh! That baby just went down for a nap. He's hollered all day," she said.

"Mama's gonna be late and I need to get Chase," I replied. She brought out two plates wrapped in cloth napkins.

"Your mama already told me, child. I made some cabbage, fried chicken, yams, and cornbread. Had plenty left. And don't wake that baby up. He ain't been feelin' well. Fever keeps coming and going. But you can come in here and help me with something 'til he wakes up."

Mama Joyce never asked anyone for anything. On that particular day, she looked really tired, so I didn't mind helping. I helped her wash dishes and fold a few loads of towels while we watched the evening news. "These damn thugs just shootin' up every damn thing. I tell you what, they bet not come on this side of town with that mess. Folks can't even walk to the store without ending up in a drive-by. Promise me you won't ever get caught up with none of them boys," she fussed.

"I promise," I replied.

Silence fell over the room as the news went to commercial. I took a deep breath and turned to her, hoping she'd be more understanding and less motherly than Mama. "Speaking of boys, I met this new boy at school. Guys usually don't even look in my direction and he followed me around all day." Mama Joyce laughed.

"Girl, it sounds like he's just looking for a friend. Ain't nothing wrong with that. But was he cute?" she asked, still laughing.

"Really cute!" I gushed. She rested her hand on my knee and said, "Just be yourself".

Then, Mama pulled into the driveway and Chase instantly woke up crying. It was like he had her on some kind of timer. I gave Mama Joyce a hug, grabbed Chase, and got back home. Mama was taking her shoes off at the door when we came in.

"Chase has a fever," I said.

She looked as if the last thing she needed was a sick baby. She took him from me and started stroking the back of his head softly. His cries died down in no time. Before taking her plate and heading to her room, she said, "I quit my job today. Don't worry. I put an ad in the paper to start my own shit".

When the door to her room closed, I knew something

deeper was going on. I didn't hear from her nor Chase again, so I ate my dinner in front of the tv in my room and wrote in my journal.

My journal was the only place I could go to collect my thoughts. It was the only way I could express my feelings without my business being spread like a wildfire through the neighborhood and school. Mama had some loose lips, so my business tended to slip whenever she was doing hair and gossiping with her clients. I just took heed and learned to keep my business to myself.

She could never know about Tremaine. I would never hear the end of it. I would get the whole *talk* again, along with some condoms that I didn't need. To Mama, having a crush equaled sex. Sex she just knew I was having. I guess she was paranoid because I didn't tell her about my first time. That was one lesson I learned the hard way.

CHAPTER 9

TREMAINE

My last shift for the week at the shop with Unc was hectic. People that didn't know nothing wanted to tell me how to do my job. One customer accused me of not giving her the correct change. Another accused me of following her around the store. Every time, my anger got the best of me and I wanted to snap, but Unc always stepped in, shoved a pacifier in their mouths and sent them on their way.

"If you can't control your emotions, you're not going to make it very far in life," he always said. The truth was that I didn't have a problem controlling my emotions. I had a problem with customers being disrespectful, acting like I owed them my kindness because I needed to make a few bucks. The old Tremaine would've been fired, but they did things differently out in California.

After the last customer left, I locked up and we started cleaning and putting stuff away. We mainly fixed computers and cell phones, but since not everybody was up on the trend, business was slow. Unc took out a business loan and started a pawn shop. We hadn't seen a bad day since he opened, which was why we couldn't leave anything sitting on the counters overnight. We couldn't afford a break-in.

I could tell the shop was Unc's pride and joy and he didn't play about his business. As tiring as it was to put stuff up and pull it right back out the next day, it was worth it. When people didn't come back to make payments on their stuff, we added to our inventory.

"Nephew, come see me in the back," he shouted.

I saw a gang of money spread across the table. He picked up a small stack and passed it to me. "You earned it," he said, not looking up from counting the rest and writing up the earnings from the day. I counted out $180 and started grinning just thinking of all the stuff I was ready to spend it on.

"Thanks, Unc."

I stuffed the money in my pocket and finished picking up around the office. When he sealed the envelope, we headed for the door, shutting off the lights over the wall where an old rug hang that had dogs playing pool on it. Unc was weird, but let him tell it, "That's going to be worth a lot of money one day, boy". On the way home, we stopped and got some grub from Fat Burger, over on Manchester. When we got back to the house, I sucked down my food and was headed for my room when I heard, "Where you going? You don't wanna talk to ya old man?"

I knew I was about to get a lecture. It was right on time, just like every other month. "I just wanted to be sure you remembered the rules around here," he said, pulling a tomato off his burger and struggling to get a sip of his vanilla shake.

"I remember. No girls in my room. School comes first. No babies. Curfew on a school night is nine o'clock. Curfew on the weekend is 11 o'clock. Wash whatever I use. No babies. No drugs. No hanging out with bad influences. And just in case you didn't hear me before, no babies!" I said, mocking him.

He sat there and laughed at me. "What's funny?" I asked. He held up a finger while he finished chewing his food.

"You probably think living here is like jail, huh?" I

nodded and leaned against the wall, because I knew he wasn't done. I had seen the inside of a jail a few times and living with him was nothin' like that. He was just annoying as hell.

"Boy, in my day, we had a whole laundry list of stuff we had to do. Your granny wasn't telling us what we couldn't do. We had so many responsibilities, we didn't have time for trouble. But your mama? She made time. She thought she knew everything. We couldn't tell her nothin'. She dropped out in 10th grade, when she thought she could take care of herself. Your brother came shortly after that. A few years later, when we thought she was getting her life together, you came along."

I had heard this story too many times to count from my granny. Mama was gone and Travis was doing time because of it. I wasn't about to end up like either of them. For some reason I couldn't convince Unc of that, though. He continued talking as my mind wandered off. When my strawberry shake settled into the pit of my stomach, I cut him off mid-sentence and locked up in the bathroom until I was sure I had flushed all my organs down the toilet.

CHAPTER 10

CARMEN

A few weeks after our big blow-up, Mami started doing more around the house and came to me about money less often. I started to feel bad, but she acted like nothing ever even happened and made sure dinner was ready every day when I got home from school.

One night, she finally made the enchiladas she promised me on the first day of school. When dinner was ready, she called me to the table. I immediately lost my appetite when I saw Elisio sitting at the head of the table. I sat down and began eating. After talking directly to Mami and looking right past him for several minutes, he finally spoke.

"You know something, Carmen? You really are a disrespectful little girl."

I almost choked on my food trying to figure out who he was talking to. I looked up at Mami who didn't say anything. She tried to grab Elisio's hand to shut him up, but he pulled away. He stood up, stuck his chest out, and proceeded to make this grand speech about how I needed to learn some respect for my elders, which I had no problem doing. But with me, respect was earned, not given, and he hadn't earned an ounce of my respect.

I looked directly into his eyes with a smug grin on my face. When somebody knocked on the door, he got quiet. That was the quietest I'd ever seen the two of them together. Nobody moved. Then, we heard the landlord shout, "I know you're in there!" Rent must have been late again. When the knocking turned into kicking Elisio stormed over to the door. Mr. Luce stood there, all of 4'11", with his potbelly hanging over a pair of oversized pants.

"I just paid you last week, man! This is bull and you know it!" Elisio shouted, making sure the entire apartment complex could hear him whining about the rent we all knew he hadn't paid.

While they stood at the door, fussing with the landlord, I saw an opportunity, to grab Mami's phone from her purse. I stuck it in my bra, cleared my plate, and went to my room. I waited until things settled before making the call. I pulled my newspaper from my backpack and dialed the number for the last job on my list.

"Hello?" a young girl's voice called out from the other end of the phone.

"I'm calling about the ad in the paper. Is the position still open?" I asked.

"Position? I'm not sure what you're talking about, and my mama's not in right now. I'll have her call you back. What's your name?

"Carmen," I said, forcing a lump back down my throat.

"Thanks, Carmen. I'll let her know you called."

When she hung up, I turned the ringer off and stuck Mami's phone under my pillow. A couple of hours later, my pillow vibrated. Through a muffled bunch of yes's and okays, I managed to secure a job and finally get back on track with my college savings. I was excited to start the next day, and even more excited to know my new boss sounded like a Black lady.

CHAPTER 11

SIOBHAN

After a disappointing first few weeks of school, Daddy picked me up for a random Saturday date that consisted of breakfast, shopping, ice cream, and a movie. We were in line at the neighborhood ice cream parlor when he started going on about boys, as always. "Don't get caught up," he always said. Then, it was, "After the first one, you know where they come from". He loved giving me a hard time about dating and relationships because he knew it made me uncomfortable and he liked to see me squirm.

He always called me his Chocolate Princess and loved telling me that I was the most beautiful girl in the world. He said it with so much assurance that I never felt invisible around him. He made me feel like I mattered. But if anybody knew how to kill the mood, it was Daddy.

"So, what's next?" he asked.

Of all people, my daddy, Nico Butler, knew I hadn't decided on a career to pursue after high school. He always preached to me about getting a good education so that I wouldn't end up like Mama. He said she had the potential to be something great, but that she didn't apply herself. He even offered to make her vice president in his up and coming cell phone company. Said it was going to be a big deal and it would've been smart to take him up on his offer before things took off. But Mama always had plans that didn't involve being tied down to any man or slaving for "the man" for the rest of her life.

Daddy fought hard to get Mama back, and she laughed in his face every time. It got to the point where he just paid child support and picked me up for his weekends with me. He would pull up every Saturday morning and blow his horn, making Mama roll her eyes at him through the blinds in the living room. He never missed a single weekend, until Shelly came along. After they met, he started getting later and later with the pickups, and eventually, he stopped coming for a few months. Turns out Shelly was no good and Daddy didn't play about loyalty.

After I got my banana split with gummy bears on top, I found us a table by the front window of the shop so we could talk and laugh at the people who passed by. "Graduation will be here before you know it," he started. I kept eating my ice cream, hoping he would change the subject. "Shanté is still gonna need your help with Chase while you figure out your life. You gave it any thought?" he asked.

"I haven't been interested in much of anything lately," I said.

"Have you tried talking to your school counselor?"

"I've been avoiding her since our meeting at the end of junior year. She is too pushy. I just don't think everyone has to have a passion in life. Like, maybe I should just take it day by day," I said.

"My baby girl is too beautiful and smart to think like that. Have you looked in the mirror lately? You are gorgeous. I'm not just saying that because I'm your daddy.

I mean it. Look at those legs...your teeth...your skin. You could be a model, girl," he said, as his ice cream started to melt and run down his hand.

"Daddy, just give me some time, please. School just started. I'll figure it out," I said, just before Tremaine walked by. My chest felt hot and heavy.

"You okay?" Daddy asked.

"Yeah, fine."

As soon as my heartbeat returned to normal, Tremaine came by again, carrying a box of shoes, heading straight for the ice cream parlor. I tried to hide my face, and it worked until he was about to leave.

"Siobhan, right?" Tremaine asked.

Daddy looked confused, looking from Tremaine to me. Then, he stood up and shook Tremaine's hand.

"Nico Butler…Siobhan's dad. How do you know my daughter?"

"Nice to meet you, sir. We met at school. I moved here from Louisiana with my uncle," Tremaine said.

"Oh, so you two go to school together?" Daddy asked, nudging me to join the conversation.

"Tremaine…hey! You left your library book the other day, at lunch," I stuttered.

"It's cool. I got it for you. Just return it when you're done. It was nice meeting you, Mr. Butler. I'll see you at school Siobhan," Tremaine said, then left.

Daddy sat down and lightly kicked my foot under the table. "Tremaine, huh? You're crushing big time. You couldn't even talk to the damn boy," Daddy said.

"Daddy, stop!" I whined. "Can we go?"

After ice cream, we went and watched a movie in the park. I didn't talk the whole ride back to the house. Daddy was playing his East Coast vs. West Coast mixtape, while my armpits were sweating. I replayed the encounter with Tremaine in my head several times, thinking about all of the things I could have said.

As we pulled up to the house, I could see Chase's little hands playing in the curtains. Then, another car pulled up behind us, and Daddy grabbed my arm as I was getting out.

"I know you get tired of walking and asking for rides everywhere, and we both know your mama needs your help. You should be getting a job soon, so I figured you'd need a car," he said.

He handed over the keys to his blue 1997 Toyota Corolla. The woman in the car behind him got out and walked up to us, extending her arms for a hug. "It's nice to finally meet you, Siobhan. I'm Debbie," she said. I accepted her warm embrace as the scent of lavender radiating from her skin calmed the thoughts racing through my head. As I pulled back to take in her short haircut and freckled skin that had this beautiful glow, I noticed Daddy was smiling hard. He winked at me and took my place in Debbie's arms. He liked this one. I could tell by the way they looked at each other.

I left them standing there making eyes at each other, hopped in my car and took it all in. Daddy leaned inside my window and took a serious tone with me.

"You earned this. But you have to work hard to keep it. Now, you can finally use that driver's license that's been in your purse collecting dust." We laughed together for a minute before I gave him a big hug and he left. I turned around and Mama was standing on the porch with Chase on her hip.

"Daddy gave me his car!" I squealed.

She put Chase down and he ran over to me. While I covered his little face in kisses, I heard Mama say, "I have a client coming over in a few. Get him fed and in the bed." She always knew how to ruin my mood.

CHAPTER 12

TREMAINE

As a young, Black man in America, I had the weight of the world on my shoulders. I was constantly reminded that nothing was ever enough and there was always room for improvement. I had to present myself in a way where society wasn't able to instantly label me as a statistic. Nah, I ain't have my moms or a daddy around, like most of the kids I knew at school. But that was part of what motivated me to keep my nose clean. Yeah, my granny had to pick up the slack for my mama most of my life, but Unc told me that didn't mean that I couldn't still grow up and become a productive member of society.

Whenever I wasn't sure about how else I could make myself more valuable and marketable in the workplace, I turned to Uncle Tony.

It just so happened that he had planned to teach me how to change the oil in his car and change a tire. I never had anybody around to teach me this kind of stuff, so it always made me feel weird inside when Unc cared enough to teach me something. As soon as we got outside, it started thundering. I could see a storm brewing in the clouds, and they moved in and covered the sun.

"We can't do this some other time, Unc? Looks like it's about to rain," I said. He shook his head and continued to the trunk of his car where he pulled out this old, dirty tire.

By the time I got the car jacked up, it started sprinkling. The rain was a refreshing feeling on my hot skin. "What you standing around for?" Unc asked.

"I just bought these khakis and now I'm about to get oil and dirt all over 'em," I said.

Unc laughed at me as I dusted the dirt off my hands. "You going to get started today?" he asked. I tried every position possible and I couldn't get a handle on the wrench. It was like somebody super glued the lug nuts on. The rain was picking up and my hands kept slipping. I was ready to give up when Unc came and shoved me out of the way.

"You about to get both of us struck by lightning

moving like molasses. Here, let me show you something," he said.

I stood back, wiping the mixture of salty sweat and rain from my forehead, and watched as Uncle Tony climbed up on the wrench and made it turn. "You have to put your body weight into it," he said. I went back over and gave it another shot, loosening a second lug nut. I was able to handle the rest on my own, but that didn't relieve me of Unc's slick jokes about "young people these days".

We were headed back up to the apartment when a jeep pulled into the parking lot. Unc knew from the way they laid on the horn that it was somebody he knew. A girl hung out of the window and shouted, "Sup, Daddy?" I looked at Unc. He looked at me, then dropped his head.

"Oh yeah, did I mention I have a daughter?" he asked.

We waited for her to get upstairs before going inside. From the way Unc kept her at a distance when hugging her, I could tell she was trouble. "Tremaine, this is my daughter, Whitney. Whitney, this is your cousin, Tremaine. This is the one I was telling you about, that's from Louisiana," he said.

We went in the house and I went straight to take a hot shower. When I got out, Whitney was at the foot of my bed, looking through my journal. I snatched it so quick, I almost broke one of her nails. "Dang, cousin. It's like that?

You got some good stuff in there. Crackhead mama issues, brother in jail…" I held the towel up around my waist and showed her to the door. Before I closed it, I got right in her face.

"Don't ever let me hear you talking about my mama or my brother. You don't know me and I don't know you. Let's keep it that way," I said.

She looked scared for a second then burst out laughing in my face. She put one of her ghetto ass nails on my temple, and said, "Don't get it twisted. We family and all, but don't get ya feelings hurt tryna be a hard ass. I mean, please. You write in a diary. Grow a pair, then step to me," she said. I let the door slam right in her face and made sure to lock it.

That was why I didn't discuss my feelings with other people, especially girls. I could trust Unc to keep my business between us, but some people just wouldn't understand. Where I came from, men couldn't have feelings. It did help with my nightmares though. When I first moved out here, I used to have the same dream every single night. It was stressful reliving seeing my mama die right in front of me. I wouldn't wish that on my worst enemy.

I was almost done getting dressed when Uncle Tony knocked on my door. When I opened it, he had his back turned to me. "Yes, sir?" I asked.

He passed a few dollars through the door and sighed heavily.

"I hope I don't regret this, but if you wanna get out and go do something, you can take my car. Just be back before dark," he said.

I got out of there before he had a chance to change his mind. I rolled up on Siobhan, but it didn't look like anybody was home. Since the rain had stopped, and I felt like riding, I did just that. I cruised the streets of L.A. and took it all in.

When I got home that night, Unc was cracking jokes about my driving. Talking about one of his homies seen me leaned all the way back like I was the shit. I could hear him laughing from the dinner table. Before I closed my eyes that night, I heard him wailing like a wounded dog on the couch. I made sure he heard me laughing all the way from my room. His one milkshake a day routine had caught up with him, and for the first time, I got the last laugh.

CHAPTER 13

CARMEN

After landing the job in the paper, I decided to start looking for back-up work. Mami was going crazy trying to figure out what happened to her phone, and I couldn't give it up just yet. She couldn't know what I was up to. She would've just gotten in the way or asked me how much I made.

After I finished hemming a slip for Ms. Marsalis, I got out and filled out applications at as many places as I could, within walking distance.

The last store I went into was a bridal store. The smell of mint and lemons met me at the entrance, as I looked around, completely amazed at the detailing and beading on some of the gowns. So many different fabrics and styles for all body types draped over the mannequins. I stood around and admired the beautiful designs, forgetting why I was even there, when a lady walked up to me. "The sign in the window says you're hiring. I was hoping to get an application," I said, eagerly. The lady looked me up and down and bumped into me as she walked over to the window to take the sign down. Then, she came back over to me and said, "My apologies. That position was filled last week. But we do have an upcoming opening for a janitor. You'd be responsible for cleaning the toilets, vacuuming, and pulling the trash after closing".

I was no stranger to hard work, and I wasn't above cleaning toilets, if that's what it took to get to where I wanted to be. But something about the way she offered the job rubbed me the wrong way. It seemed like she thought I was desperate or that I didn't know how to do anything else. I wasn't interested in sales. I wanted to fix the dresses after the brides lost or gained too much weight before their weddings.

I left there with my heart in my hands, but I wasn't ready to give up. The sun was setting, and I knew I had to get home before all of the creatures took over the parking lot. I hated walking home and being subjected to a bunch of men hanging out in their cars, smoking and drinking, undressing me with their eyes.

I got upstairs to our apartment just before the streetlights came on and there was a note on our door. Mami and Elisio still hadn't managed to come up with the rent money and the landlord was threatening to evict us, again. As bad as I wanted to pay the rent for Mami, I knew it would be a waste of my hard-earned money because that same notice would be right back on the door in a couple of weeks when rent would be due again.

That was a chance I was willing to take. If it came down to it, we'd need a hotel room or somewhere else to stay. If I paid for it, then I could tell Mami I didn't want Elisio there. When I walked in, they were dancing in the living room, while a cigarette hung from the corner of Elisio's mouth. "Come on, mija. Join us!" Mami said.

"No, thanks," I replied. I grabbed a few snacks from the kitchen and locked up in my room for the rest of the night.

With my sketchpad in my lap, I vomited all of the ideas that had floated around in my head all week, with one of Selena's albums playing softly, in the background. My sketchpad was full of designs and I just knew that if the right person saw them, all of my dreams would come true. Mami always told me that I was ahead of my time with my designs, and that if I was keeping up with the current trends, I would always be behind. So, I decided to become a trendsetter.

CHAPTER 14

SIOBHAN

As fourth period ended, I headed straight for the cafeteria and got in line. I had looked forward to this day since the lunch menu for that month came out. Nacho salad was the only thing they served that I actually liked. Everything else looked and tasted like garbage. I had to eat inside because of the storm, and I was headfirst in my food, with cheese dripping from my lip when Tremaine walked up on me from behind and whispered in my ear, "Sup?"

A chip got stuck in my throat on the way down and I couldn't breathe. I began to panic while everyone around me watched in fear as I blacked out. The next thing I knew, Tremaine's arms were around my chest and he was attempting to administer the Heimlich Maneuver. Moments later, the chip dislodged, and I could breathe again. My throat burned and my chest hurt, but I was alive. Everyone stood around, staring, and gossiping, but none of them checked on me. They were too busy high fiving Tremaine for saving my life.

While everyone was singing his praises, I was forced to go to the nurse's office by a teacher. Tremaine went with me and finished his lunch while I got checked out. They called Mama, who insisted on coming to pick me up, but I refused to go home. I had a test in English that I couldn't miss. Plus, the senior assembly and pep rally was at the end of the day.

About 30 minutes later, I was released back to class, where Tremaine had saved me a seat. Somehow, he had managed to get a schedule exactly like mine. Over time, I realized there wasn't anywhere in school we didn't go together.

After the last bell rang, he asked if I could have company. Without a second thought, I answered, "Yeah". As we walked toward the parking lot, he began to look confused.

"You got a car?" he asked while getting in, touching everything.

"My daddy got it for me the same day we ran into each other at the ice cream parlor."

"That's cool. Seems like all the seniors drive, except me," he said, turning to look out the window, as his tone changed.

"It's okay. I can drive you every day if you want. Where do you live?"

"About 20 minutes away, in some white apartments. I can just meet you…"

"You don't know the address?" I asked. He paused, and looked at me, shrugging his shoulders. "Look, don't sweat it. I got you. Just be ready around seven every morning," I said.

When we pulled up to the house, I was already nervous, knowing Mama would kill me if she caught me with another boy in the house. I looked around and saw Mama Joyce in her living room window, watching us. I thought that since Mama was always late, I would have him gone before she got there. My plan folded and my life flashed before my eyes when I heard her pull up in the driveway in the middle of a rerun of *Martin*. I jumped out of my bed, threw Tremaine a book and we pretended to be studying.

"Let me guess. You didn't ask if I could come over…"

Before I could answer, the front door slammed and I

could hear her on the way to my room. Tremaine sat calmly on the floor and I sat up in my bed, legs crossed, head down. She stuck her head in, looked around, then stepped back out in the hallway.

"I'll be right back," I said.

My heart was racing, and I just knew he could hear it. Mama put the fear of God in everybody. Everybody knew not to play with Shanté Butler.

"You wanna tell me why you have a boy in your bedroom, again?" she asked.

"He came over to study. We had to choose a book to write a report on and we're doing dual perspectives of *The Color Purple*. I'm doing Mister and he's doing Celie. I didn't think you would mind. We just got here. He lives like 10 minutes from here," I said, still scared she was about to smack fire from me.

She bit her lip, looked up to the ceiling and just walked away. I think I even heard her laugh, so I knew it was time for him to go. It was hard not to, but a smile spread across my face. Yeah, I felt bad, but then again, I felt *bad*.

"Go get Chase!" she yelled, as she closed her bedroom door. Something didn't feel right, so I knocked lightly then stuck my head in the door. She was sitting on the side of the bed with her head hung low.

"How was work?" I asked.

She didn't acknowledge my question or my presence. She began to undress and turned on some music and lit a bunch of candles. I let her be and left to get Chase. As I turned my back, I heard her say, "I quit my job

I was so relieved when we pulled into the parking lot of Tremaine's apartments. It was super awkward when he was getting out. Then, once he closed the door, he leaned back into the window and said, "We should hang out again sometime."

"Yeah. That's cool," I said, counting the seconds until he was inside and I was cleared to freak out.

CHAPTER 15

CARMEN

It had been storming for days on end. Usually, the rain didn't bother me. But while sitting in English class, I felt something drip on my forehead and roll down my cheek. I looked up and the ceiling looked like it was going to collapse at any moment. After another drop of water fell, I raised my hand to ask for permission to change seats. Before I could gather my stuff, the most disgusting brown water burst through the tiled ceiling and splashed everywhere. My hair and clothes were ruined. My mascara was running, and I was soaked. Everybody else managed to stay dry and watched and laughed as I rang my clothes out in a nearby puddle.

I looked at Mrs. Wooten and she nodded toward the

door. I grabbed my stuff and headed for the restroom, rushing to the sink to check and clean up my face and hair. I could hear a lot of movement from the handicap stall and two people fussing, trying desperately to whisper. I turned around just as the door swung open. André and the quiet, shy girl of our class, Bethany, walked out, fixing their clothes. He looked like he'd seen a ghost and she looked like she just wanted to disappear. I turned back around and pulled all my hair up, reapplied my makeup, and left.

André was waiting on me outside of the restroom and grabbed my arm as I headed back to class. "Don't touch me!" I shouted and punched him in his chest. As I walked away, I could hear him coughing, trying to catch his breath. Nothing in me cared enough to go back and check on him either.

As soon as school was over that day, I ran to catch the bus for my first day of work. The address my new boss had given me was out in Beverly Hills. The bus only went so far, then I had to walk the rest of the way. I ended up being late, but she didn't give me a hard time about it. She just threw me a uniform, told me to change and get to work. The house was massive, so I knew we would be there for a while, but I didn't mind. Anywhere was better than where I lived.

A bunch of old ass paintings covered the walls, along with some hideous wallpaper that was starting to peel. It smelled like an old lady's perfume, and the only thing that was halfway nice was the chandelier in the entryway.

We were careful not to break anything and stayed out of rooms where the doors were closed. The only time Ms. Shanté spoke to me was when I was doing something wrong, like taking out the trash. We didn't just change the trash bags. We were expected to put a new one underneath the replacement, along with a dryer sheet, so that the trash can didn't stink, and there was always the convenience of a replacement being on hand until we came back, because God forbid the owners did anything for themselves..

Ms. Shanté turned on the owner's old record player while we cleaned. She told me to bring a headset the next time, but that it was okay that I didn't that day because the owners had just left for London and wouldn't be back for the next two months.

When we started wrapping up for the night, the silence that filled the home was unbearable. I stood to the side, with two big trash bags, as Ms. Shanté sat at the large dining room table and massaged the soles of her feet.

"I know I should've asked before hiring you, but I needed the help. Does your mom know where you are?" she asked.

I had to think of a lie and quick, but as soon as I tried to feed it to her, her facial expression changed, and my lie turned into the truth.

"I need the money for college. I want to be a fashion designer, but all of the best schools are expensive."

"I wish you were my kid. My daughter still don't know what she wants to do, and I'm scared she's gonna end up somewhere living off of government assistance for the rest of her life. She is not motivated to do anything but watch tv," she said, sighing, as she rested her head on the back of the chair, closing her eyes.

It felt weird having an adult vent to me about her kid, but it also felt good having someone to listen to me for a change.

"I'm sure she'll figure it out," I said, creating even more awkward silence. "Is this your dream? Cleaning houses for rich people?" I asked.

"I wanted to be a beautician, but my mama talked me out of it. She said, "There's no money in doing hair", and that it's a service people want, and didn't need. I listened to her and ended up working for a man who couldn't even remember my name after 10 years. I quit right after I hired you."

We walked and talked while making all lights were out and doors were locked on our way out. As I got to the end of the driveway, I heard her yell, "Where are you going?"

"I caught the bus here," I responded.

"Come on here. You're not getting on a bus this late

at night," she said.

She took me home and walked me to the front door, past all of the creeps lingering in the parking lot who were yelling and whistling at us. When I turned the key to unlock the door, it swung open and Mami stood there with her hands on her hips, fuming.

"¿Dónde has estado? ¡He estado preocupado por ti toda la noche!" she yelled.

I turned to Ms. Shanté and hugged her. "Thank you," I said. She held me tightly and kissed me at the top of my head. Mami kept going on and on, so loud her voice was echoing throughout the complex. Once Ms. Shanté was out of sight and the door was closed, she let me have it.

"What the hell are you doing hanging out with that bitch? I was worried sick about you! You don't just come home late and not tell me. I'm your mother, not her!"

"I KNOW," I shouted. "You remind me every damn day! I got a job so I could get the hell out of here."

Mami about choked on her next sentence because she couldn't say anything else. She just pointed to my bedroom. I gladly closed and locked my door. To tune her out, I did my daily recount of my stash, but I could still hear her fussing in Spanish, pacing back and forth near my door. Then, I noticed I was missing a few twenty-dollar bills. Everything in me wanted to confront her, but I knew she would just lie her way out of it.

For the next week, I went to work with Ms. Shanté, cleaning houses, and office buildings. It started to feel less like work because she was so cool to hang around. We would have little dance party breaks, and she gave me all kinds of unsolicited advice about boys. She even invited me over for dinner to meet her daughter. I didn't have any friends, so I wasn't opposed to the idea. Just didn't want to have to hear Mami's mouth because it was clear that something went down between the two of them years ago, and Mami wasn't letting up about it.

CHAPTER 16

SIOBHAN

Every day after school, Tremaine came over to hang out. We would change the channel back and forth between *The Wayans Brothers*, *Martin* and *Moesha* until it hurt us to laugh. He was easy to get along with. It seemed like he did just want a friend. During a commercial break, I grabbed a couple of sodas and chips from the kitchen. In the time that I was gone, Tremaine had taken off his shoes, climbed up in my bed, and laid back, with his hands behind his head.

"What are you doing? You can't be in my bed!" I said. "If my mama saw you..."

"Relax, girl. I was just tired of sitting on the floor. Can I have my drink, please?" he asked.

He sat up at the foot of the bed and drank his soda, slurping super loud. I could tell he was uncomfortable, and I was embarrassed about the way I had reacted before. Because of that, things were weird for the rest of that evening. Then, when we left to take him home, I stopped by to pick up Chase and Mama Joyce laid into me.

"Who is this boy that you keep bringing home with you? Did you not learn from the last time? Boys ain't nothing but trouble."

"That's the boy I was telling you about. We're just friends, Mama Joyce. I promise!" I said.

"He's just a friend that you like…a lot. What happens when he starts to like you too? You have protection? You know how to control yourself?"

I started to take offense to her comments, so I grabbed Chase and left. On the way to Tremaine's house, the two of them got way too hype listening to *The Rugrats Movie* soundtrack. I had never seen Chase take to anyone like that and he seemed to like Tremaine a lot.

When we pulled up, I assumed we would continue our usual routine. He would take his time getting out while trying to start up some sort of conversation. But this time he invited me in. I instantly got hot in the collar, and looked back at Chase, hoping he was falling asleep. He was wide awake and reaching for me. Tremaine's smile made it hard to tell him no, so we went inside. Their place was pretty neat to say men lived there. Mama always said men were naturally nastier than women, and that "It's just how we're made".

"Unc, I'm home. Siobhan is here too," he yelled.

His uncle, Tony, came from the back of the apartment and checked on the food on the stove. Then, he came to shake my hand. "It's nice to finally meet you, Siobhan. My nephew has told me a lot about you. He's been a gentleman, I hope?"

"He's been a perfect gentleman," I replied, smiling and nudging Tremaine.

"Who is this little man right here? Hey there little guy," he said, trying to shake Chase's hand.

I smiled politely as Chase started getting fussy. I was beyond relieved to have the perfect excuse to leave. "TJ, walk your company out," he said.

"Yes, sir," Tremaine replied.

While walking me to my car, Chase calmed down. "See you tomorrow?" I just smiled and buckled my seatbelt as he closed my door. He stood to the side and watched us pull away. I watched him through the rearview mirror until we turned the corner. The nighttime breeze and slow jams on the radio calmed my nerves as I took my time getting home.

CHAPTER 17

TREMAINE

Whenever things started to get to me and I wasn't sure if Unc could understand what I was going through, it was almost always time for a fresh haircut. The fellas at the shop always had two cents to offer about what I should do about any given situation. I had to get cleaned up for my senior yearbook picture, so we had to go see my man, Big Ronnie, over on South Main.

Big Ronnie was the man, back in the day. I could tell there was some type of history with him and Uncle Tony that was off limits to discuss. Everybody always got quiet when we walked in.

That day, everybody was in a good mood. "Heeeey, Big T! My man," Big Ronnie would say, as he waited for his last client to pay him. These guys were some high rollers. Everywhere you looked, they had on the latest Gucci, FUBU, Reebok and even Rolex's. Dudes would pull out a big old bankroll, just to pay $20 for a cut.

I walked right in and climbed in the chair, hoping Unc wouldn't get them all hyped up about the non-sense between me and Siobhan again. There was nothing there, but friendship. Her attitude made me look at her a little differently, and she wasn't as nice as I thought she was, so I backed off. I couldn't get them to see that though. "Hey Lil' T. How's things with ya little girlfriend?" Papa Jessie asked. He was the oldest in the shop. Had it passed down to him from his dad, who got it from his dad.

"I told y'all, man. Siobhan is not my girlfriend. We're just friends," I said, making sure to drop my voice a few octaves so they'd take me seriously. Uncle Tony sat in the chair across from me, waiting his turn, raising his eyebrows every time I mentioned her name. He kept his head down, reading a hair magazine, pretending not to be ear hustling.

He looked like he'd swallowed a canary when Big Ronnie said, "Man, you yo uncle's nephew. When I met him, he was crazy behind this fine young thang. What was her name, Tonio? Oh, oh, I remember now. It was Natalie! Boy,

Natalie had that boy head gone. He tried to convince us they was just friends too. Now they got a bratty ass daughter who gives 'em both a run for their money."

"Nah, Big Ron. It wasn't even like that. She played me. Y'all knew that girl was already pregnant when I met her," Unc said.

"Wait, Whitney not yours?" I asked.

Big Ronnie smacked the back of my head. "Boy, you don't ask no man his business like that. What's wrong with you?" he fussed.

I was confused. They felt good enough to ask me all my business like it was in the news or something. I sucked my teeth and let my head down so Big Ronnie could catch the back.

"Well, all I know is, I don't have no babies and I ain't makin' none. Not right now, anyway," I said, hoping they'd lay off of me. Big Ronnie smacked my head again with a handful of alcohol. I thought I would've been used to it by then, but it felt like he used more than the usual amount that time. Everything in me wanted to knock his head off.

"Gone now, youngblood. Sit on over there and let me get my boy," he said.

Still rubbing the back of my neck, I moved to the side and let Unc climb in the chair. Every time he got up there, Big Ronnie would grip his shoulders really tight and say something really low, next to Unc's ear. I could tell by the way Uncle Tony would clench his jaw that whatever it was, wasn't good.

"Aye, aye, Tremaine. Let's see that pose for the yearbook," Papa Jessie shouted. All eyes were on me and I was feeling myself after Big Ronnie lined up my 'stache. I strolled down the middle of the walkway, posed, gave the girls passing by the windows a lil' smooch, then turned and pimp walked back to my seat. I smiled real big and everybody laughed at me.

"You smile like that in that yearbook and you and Siobhan's kids gone be laughing at you for the rest of ya life," Big Ronnie said.

"Man, y'all really don't understand what just friends mean, huh?" I asked, laughing.

They all looked at each other and fell out laughing again. "What's funny?" I asked.

"Nothing, man. They just messing around," Unc said.

When he was done with his cut, Big Ronnie led him to the back for a few minutes and when they came out, he was in a hurry to leave. I didn't question it. He always told me to stay out of his business, so I did.

On the way home, it kept playing over and over in my mind about what the guys in the shop said. A girl and a boy could be just friends, right? I looked over at Unc, trying to gain the courage to talk to him about how I was feeling and what I was thinking. That jaw was still clenched, and he was red in the face, so I turned the radio up and kept my thoughts to myself, that time.

CHAPTER 18

CARMEN

Once things began to cool down again between me and
Mami, she started hanging around my room, trying to spend
time with me. While I was working on a pair of slacks for a
customer, she came in and laid across my bed and opened
this bridal magazine. She flipped over on her back and began
circling the most expensive dresses she came across.

"I'm so happy you can sew and have an eye for
design. I can cut my dress budget down and save the money
for our honeymoon. How many moms can say that? Right?"
she asked, laughing.

Instead, I stopped sewing and grabbed the magazine
from her, looking closely at the dresses she was admiring.

"Are you serious about marrying him? Mami, he's no good for you. He can't even keep a job," I said.

She sat up and paused before responding. "Why can't I get married, Carmen? Why can't I have the kind of life I've always dreamed of? Elisio is good for me. He doesn't cheat. He even wants to work on his relationship with you. He told me so," she lied.

"Mami, I want you to have everything you've ever wanted. I know you sacrificed a lot for me…for us. But I do not like, nor do I trust him. You shouldn't have to ask your kid for money to pay the bills when you have a man living with you."

Mami got up and headed for the door. "Thanks for the support," she said before turning and bumping into Elisio in the hallway. I went back to what I was doing, hoping that was the end of that conversation. About an hour later, I was heading to the kitchen for a snack, and he blocked my doorway.

"Going somewhere?" he asked, wearing a disgusting grin on his face. He caressed the side of my face with his dirty hands, as spit filled the corners of his mouth.

"Move out of my way," I said, trying to push him away from me.

He laughed, flashing a mouthful of gold and dirty, rotten teeth. "Your mama told me what you said to her. One day, we're gonna be a big happy family, and you're just gonna have to accept it. You don't have to like me…"

Before he could finish his sentence, I smacked his hand away from my face. He grinned, sucked his teeth and then walked away.

"I'm not done with you," he said as he retreated to Mami's bedroom.

I grabbed my food and ran back to my room, with a knife in hand, that I stuck underneath my mattress. My nerves were all over the place and suddenly, I no longer had an appetite. I went back to sewing, hoping to forget about everything that had happened earlier. My eyes were getting heavy and I was dozing off when a knock at my bedroom door startled me and I jumped up, grabbed my knife and walked over. "Who is it?" I asked.

"I just wanted to tell you goodnight, mija. I love you," Mami said.

"Yeah…me too," I replied, breathing a sigh of relief.

I could tell she was still out there, lingering. Her shadow finally disappeared from under the door after a few seconds, but I stood there until I heard her door close.

During a long, hot shower, I heard what sounded like a hammer hitting a wall, like somebody was hanging a picture. I took my time getting out, hoping to leave the two of them with nothing but cold water, then I snuck back down the hallway to my room and ran into Elisio, who was still grinning from ear to ear and dancing while eating a plate of leftovers.

I locked myself inside my room for the night and slept with my hand under my pillow, holding my knife. I had an eerie feeling that something bad was going to happen, so I kept my shoes by my bed and pulled out my clothes for the next day.

I had a hard time falling asleep, and when I had finally dozed off for good, the front door slammed, rattling my bedroom walls and window. My alarm clock and the air conditioner shut off abruptly. I tried to go back to sleep but I was starting to sweat and feel sick to my stomach. I was almost back asleep when I started to hear a popping noise. Then, it sounded like somebody was crumbling wads of paper outside of my door.

With sleep in my eyes, I went to see what was going on and burned myself on my door handle. Then, the heat began to radiate through the crack at the bottom of my door, followed by a thick cloud of smoke.

"Mami?" I shouted.

She didn't respond so I kept calling out. "Mami! Mami, wake up! Mami!" I screamed and banged on the door, as my room gradually filled with smoke. After a few minutes of calling out for her, I began to choke. I couldn't breathe.

My eyes were burning, and I could feel my body growing weaker. I grabbed the blanket from my bed and covered myself and the doorknob.

A wave of heat hit me as I opened my door to see the living room completely engulfed in flames. While there was still a small path to the front door, I knew I couldn't just leave her behind. I could hear the sirens from the fire truck getting closer, so I ran to the bathroom, wet as much of my blanket as I could, and covered myself back up as I tried to break Mami's door down. I felt a sharp pain in my shoulder as I ran into her door one last time, breaking the frame and falling on the floor. The smoke filled her room fast and made it hard to see and breathe. I covered my nose and mouth and felt my way around, stubbing my toe on the corner of her bed. Then, I saw her on the floor between the wall and her bed.

Her eyes were nearly swollen shut and she had blood around her mouth and ears. "Mami, get up. Please! I'm sorry! Please get up!" I cried. I started trying to drag her to the front door, but she was too heavy. Then, I ran back to my room, to my window. I banged and screamed, "Help us!"

I could see our neighbors standing around watching our apartment burn as I burned the tips of my fingers trying to open my window. There were nails in each corner, near the locks that weren't there before that day. I began to feel dizzy, so I stuck on my tennis shoes and ran back toward the hallway when I noticed my closet door was open. As I got closer, I could see my stash box on the floor, open, and empty. My heart sank.

As much as I wanted to freak out, I knew I had to get out of there. I was throwing a bag of clothes across my shoulder when I heard the fire department trying to break down the front door. "In here!" I said, gasping for air. At the sound of the last BOOM, I dropped to my knees and blacked out.

CHAPTER 19

SIOBHAN

After meeting Tremaine's uncle, he acted like everything was fine, but I felt like we needed to talk. Every time I got ready to bring it up, he would start talking about something random. This time, it was football. "Unc said it's cool if I go to the homecoming game with you. I know we didn't talk about it, but you wanna go?"

I muted the tv and asked, "Why did you want me to meet your uncle?" His nostrils flared up as he raised his eyebrow.

"He asked to meet you since we been hanging out so much. That's all," he said.

I wanted to believe there was more to it than that, but

he seemed irritated, so I turned the tv back up and left. "I'll be back," I shouted.

I needed some fresh air and picking Chase up was a great excuse to get out and be alone, even if it was just for a minute. But by the time I got back across the street, Mama's car was in the driveway. My school lunch was ready to come up at any minute, so I sped up, hoping she hadn't embarrassed me in front of Tremaine, or worse. When I walked in the door and saw him helping her put away groceries, I put Chase down in front of some cartoons and went to help.

She was talking to Tremaine like they were best friends. "Siobhan, Tremaine here is planning to study computers in college next year. You probably could learn a thing or two from him," she said. Tremaine looked at me but when I didn't acknowledge him, he went back to putting canned goods in the cabinets.

"Mama, some people just don't know what they want to do right out of high school. Besides, I have other things on my plate that I have to think about right now," I said.

I zoned out while staring at Chase as he giggled at Tommy Pickles stumbling around with a diaper on his head. I didn't hear anything else that was said until Mama shoved me. "I know you hear me talking to you," she fussed.

"Tremaine, you ready to go home?" I asked.

"If you were listening to anything I just said, you would have heard me say he's staying for dinner. Show him where the phone is so he can call and invite his uncle," Mama said.

I did as I was told and headed to my room for a few minutes to myself when there was a knock at the front door. I met Mama near the back of the couch, as we exchanged looks, trying to confirm who was at our door, without letting them know we were indeed home but didn't want to be bothered. When the knocking continued, I grabbed the steel bat that Mama kept behind the door and stood in its place while she opened it.

She didn't speak at first. She just stood to the side. Then, I saw the woman and girl from the store who pushed her. I clenched the bat tighter, praying I wouldn't have to use it. "Put the bat down, Siobhan," Mama said. I stood the bat back in its corner and everyone moved around the couch and sat down. Two bags were left at the door.

Normally, Mama would tell me to go find something to do when grown folks were talking, but not this time. "Siobhan, this is Carmen and her mom, Daya. Carmen works for me and Daya and I used to be friends when we were pregnant with you two."

"It was a long time ago," Ms. Daya said, readjusting herself on the couch as if something Mama said struck a nerve.

"Ms. Butler, I know you and my mom have some type of history, and I know it's not my business, but I was hoping you all could put that to the side for now. Our apartment caught on fire a few nights ago and we don't have anywhere else to go," Carmen said. Ms. Daya interrupted and stood back up.

"We just need one night until there's room for us at the shelter. But I don't want to be in the way, so if you would just let Carmen stay, I can make other arrangements for myself."

Mama went down the hallway and came back with a stack of blankets and pillows. "Daya, you can take the couch, for now. Carmen, you can sleep with Siobhan, in her room. There's space for your things in the hall closet," Mama said. "Dinner will be ready soon."

Mama and I were headed back into the kitchen to cook when there was another knock at the door. Daya and Carmen jumped up from the couch and moved closer to the kitchen as Mama opened the door again. Tremaine appeared from the hallway and a smile spread across his face. "What's up, Unc?" he asked, as they shared a masculine hug.

He introduced his uncle and my mama to each other, and she just smiled.

"This is Carmen and her mom, Daya. They will be

staying with us for a little while," she said.

Mama was being unusually pleasant. She was never this cool about having company over. When Tremaine's uncle spoke, Mama's demeanor changed, then he kissed her hand and I watched as her knees almost buckled.

"Antonio Johnson…It's a pleasure to meet you," he said. After that I was tasked with serving snacks and "beverages" until dinner was ready while Mama put on a show for company. Then, Tremaine and I went back to my room to finish watching our shows. "You're not gonna invite her in here?" he asked.

"I don't know her," I said, hoping to avoid the obvious conversation of how I didn't want another girl around my future boyfriend.

When dinner was served, we only had enough room at the table for four people, so Mama, Mr. Tony, and Ms. Daya sat at the table and sent me, Carmen and Tremaine to sit on the floor in the living room. She had finally taken the plastic covers off her sofas, and she cringed every time we sat on it.

Dinner was so quiet that I could hear everyone chewing. It was driving me insane. So, to break the ice, I tried to get to know Carmen.

"What happened? If you don't mind me asking…"

"I don't want to talk about," she responded, dropping

her head. Her chewing slowed as she wiped a few tears from her cheeks.

"When my mama and granny died, my Uncle Tony taught me that it's okay to cry…but when you're done, you have to pick your head up and move forward because the days behind you have nothing on the days ahead of you," Tremaine said.

That made her cry even more. Not knowing how to console her, Tremaine stuck his hand out and said, "I'm Tremaine. I'm new in town. I don't have any friends here, except for Siobhan. I could use one more."

Her cries turned into laughter as Carmen reached out to shake his hand. "Y'all not about to keep laughing at me," he said, pulling us in for a big bear hug. Carmen's face cleared up and she went back to eating her fried chicken. She managed to squeeze out an "Oh my God," every few seconds.

"Mami can cook, but not like this!" she said. We all laughed as I took mine and Tremaine's plates to the kitchen. When I came back, Carmen was getting up with half a plate of food remaining.

"You're full?" I asked.

"Just saving some for tomorrow," she said, smiling, lowering her head again.

Mama walked up behind me and reached around to

lift Carmen's head. "You don't have to worry about food here. Between Chase and his snacks, and Siobhan's picky eating, there's always something to eat," Mama said.

"Your son is really cute, Ms. Shanté," Carmen said, smiling as Chase ran up to her with his dirty little hands stretched out for her to pick him up.

Mama's smile faded as she quickly blocked the attack and swung Chase into my arms. "Bath and bedtime, now," she said. Before I took Chase to the back, Mr. Tony came from the kitchen, stretching and rubbing his belly.

"Well, Mrs. Butler," he said.

"It's miss," Mama interrupted.

"My apologies, Ms. Butler. Dinner was great. Maybe next time I can have you over to my place?" Uncle Tony continued.

Tremaine stood behind him, flailing his arms in the air, begging us not to accept the offer, loudly whispering, "Don't do it!"

While Chase was in his bath playing with his toy sharks and rubber duckies, Carmen leaned in the doorway, smiling.

"What?" I asked and Chase splashed water and bubbles in my face.

"I always wondered what it was like to have a little sister or brother. Girl, you got it pretty good up in here," she said.

As she sat patiently at the foot of my bed, I couldn't help but wonder what her life was like before the fire. After getting Chase dressed, I took him to my room to show Carmen where to put her things and gave her a set of towels.

"I'll be back once I get him to sleep. The water gets really hot, so be careful."

I wasn't sure if it was the sound of the shower running for nearly 30 minutes or Chase's mobile that he would not let us get rid of, but as soon as I laid on the floor next to his bed I fell asleep, holding his tiny hand.

CHAPTER 20

CARMEN

Mami and Abuela always instilled in me to try and figure out my problems on my own, so when Mami refused to call any of her friends from work to ask for help I decided to act. The last thing I wanted was to ask my new boss if we could come stay with her, but I also knew Mami was planning to stay at a homeless shelter. I told her that if we did, I would run away and never come back. The last time we had to stay in a shelter, a creepy homeless man almost took me in the middle of the night.

Because of the seriousness of her injuries and smoke inhalation, the doctor insisted on keeping her for 48 hours for observation. I spent those 48 hours trying to tune out the world.

But when 48 hours turned into 72 and Mami couldn't fake the pain anymore, the nurse came in to discuss being discharged. Mami faked sleep. They gave her a few more hours for the medicine to wear off, so I took the liberty of calling the only person I could think of to ask for help. When she didn't answer, I tried not to panic. I hoped she would call back since I had missed three days of work. I had lost Mami's cell phone days before the fire and I was too afraid to call off of work after having started only a few weeks prior.

I was watching the morning news and tearing into my eggs and potatoes when the room phone rang loudly. It woke Mami up, so I knew I had to come up with a plan, and fast. "I got it, Ma. Probably just the wrong room," I lied. With her eyes barely open, she motioned for me to come closer until my face was next to her mouth. Then, she quickly leaned up and kissed my cheek, and laid back down.

"Te amo, mija," she said. "Lo siento mucho… Para todo."

When the phone stopped ringing, I could feel my heart burst into a million pieces. Mami sat up in the bed and started pulling the covers back. "You need to get to school," she said, as she climbed down.

"I can miss one day, right? They'll understand. Plus, we have to find somewhere to live and I might not even be going back to that school anyway," I said, hoping to butter her up enough to let me stay with her for the day.

"Don't push your luck," she replied, as a light chuckle escaped her lips.

When Mami came back out of the bathroom, I was in bed, in her place. She stood over me and pulled the covers back, again. I moved over in the bed and patted the space I had cleared for her to lie down with me.

I laid my head in her chest, listening to the rhythm of her heartbeat, nearly falling back asleep as she ran her fingers through my hair. Just as I was drifting off, the phone rang again. I climbed back down and ran over before it stopped ringing. "Who is that?" Mami mouthed to me. I shrugged my shoulders, pretending to be confused, then I picked up. I turned my back and spoke softly so she couldn't read my lips or hear what I was saying.

"Mami, that hurt!" I shouted when the lid to her breakfast container met the center of my back. "Thank you. We'll be over later today. We just have a few things to do first," I said, then hung up the phone.

When I turned back around, Mami was halfway dressed and ripping through the plastic bag the hospital gave us. "They gave me everything but a toothbrush," she fussed.

"Ma, I'm sure they have some around here somewhere," I said as she left for the nurse's desk in her hospital gown and a pajama pants. "Get me one too!" I shouted.

I knew that as badly as Mami didn't want me to ask Ms. Shanté for help, I had to be smart about it. We were homeless, again, with barely two outfits between the two of us.

While she was out looking for a toothbrush, I ran back over to the phone. As soon as someone picked up, Mami walked back into the room and I slammed the receiver down.

"What are you up to?" Mami asked.

I grabbed the bag and headed toward the door. "No toothbrushes?" I asked.

She pulled a travel-sized tube of toothpaste from behind her back and passed it to me. "Use your finger," she said. After brushing our teeth with washcloths in silence, we rolled up the hospital linen on the bed and stuffed it in the plastic bags they gave us. Mami's face was red the entire time, as she packed as much stuff as she could find to take. The toilet tissue and a set of towels were the last two things we grabbed before stopping.

My bag was bursting at the seams. We casually strolled past the nurse's station, waving and smiling as we quietly counted our steps to the nearest exit. I could feel the sweat seeping from my forehead. We moved so fast, the only time I had to catch my breath was on our elevator ride down. As we neared the last set of doors, a woman's voice called out from behind us. "Hey!"

Mami and I sped up, hoping to get out of there and run until we were out of sight. But Mami's nurse caught us at the door.

"I know I'm not supposed to do this, but I couldn't help myself. I asked a few of the other nurses on our floor to pitch in and we pulled together a few dollars to help you all on your new journey. We know you lost everything, and we just wanted to help as much as we could," she said, grabbing Mami's hand, trying not to cry.

When the nurse stepped back, Mami opened her hand to a few twenties and fives. The nurse leaned back in and whispered, "If you need to eat later, head over to the soul food diner on La Brea, and my brother, Charles, will take care of you, on the house. Just tell him Dorothy sent you."

Mami hugged the nurse and released a heaping amount of emotions. Before we parted ways, the nurse told me, "If you ever need anything at all, you know where to find me. Take care of each other, sweetie".

When we stepped outside of the hospital doors, Mami grabbed my hand. We found the closest bus stop and just rode around the city for hours. She was hoping to find a shelter that had room for us, but every stop disappointed her more than the last.

On our last stop, we were turned away from a shelter because the line had already closed for the day. We walked across the street to the nearest park and rested on a nearby bench until most of the families had gone home. "What now?" I asked. Mami didn't respond. She was lost in her thoughts, picking apart a sweaty burger she had been carrying around since we had lunch. "Ma!" I said, bumping her leg.

"I hear you. I don't know," she said.

"Where are we gonna sleep?" I asked.

Mami pulled the money from her pocket that she got from the hospital. She counted it three times…something she often did when she was unbelievably broke and hoped she had just overlooked a few extra dollars.

"We have about $100," she said.

A lump filled the lower half of my throat as I dug deep to find the courage to suggest the unthinkable. It was time for dinner and my stomach had been talking to me for the past two hours. "I have an idea," I mumbled, as I saw a bus approaching. "Come on!" I said, pulling Mami from the bench and jetting for the bus. The doors had just closed when we made it and the driver was starting to pull away. We ran alongside the bus, beating on the doors, screaming, "Wait!"

When the driver stopped and opened the doors, Mami started going through the money in her pockets. The driver looked at us both and said, "Go on. Find a seat." We sat near the back doors and rode across the city while watching the sun disappear on the horizon. When the driver got to her last stop, I said a quick prayer to myself and we started on our way.

"Where are we going?" Mami asked. I didn't have the heart to lie to her. After all we had been through that week, telling her would ruin the surprise. Although, I was pretty sure it wouldn't be the surprise she was probably hoping for.

As we approached the house, my hunger pains turned into a ball of nerves. "Where are we?" Mami asked. I was tired of her questions, but I knew she wouldn't try to kill me in front of the Butlers, so I knocked and stepped back.

CHAPTER 21

SIOBHAN

When Mama told me that Carmen and her mom would be staying with us for a while, I knew that meant she would have to go to school with me. Mama made me call Daddy to get him to pull a few strings to get her in.

Pulliam Prep was not like other schools. It was kind of like a private school, but with the feel of a public school. We had tuition, no uniforms, free lunches for everyone, and a great curriculum.

Of course, since I drove to school, Carmen caught a ride. She sat in the backseat and looked out the window as Tremaine played with the radio, trying to find a station with no static.

"California Love" by Tupac, came on and I could see Carmen through my rearview mirror, bobbing her head. Everyone was jamming and the mood in the car changed. Tremaine started tried to rap and completely butchered the song. But I let him think he had skills because he was so cute.

As we pulled into the parking lot, all eyes were on us. We walked through the front doors of Pulliam Prep like a scene out of a movie where the *it girls* walked in and everyone's mouths hit the floor. Brandy was never without a smart comment when she saw me, but the sight of Carmen spooked her.

I could hear the whispers as we walked Carmen to her homeroom class. Before we left her, Carmen turned to us like she wanted to say something. Instead, she smiled and went on. Tremaine and I proceeded to our homeroom class to find our seats had been taken by Brandy and her football jock boyfriend, Cody. The only open seats were separated and across the room from each other. Tremaine took the seat closest to the teacher's desk and left me sitting right under the intercom speaker. My ears bled as we listened to the morning announcements. When our eyes locked, he laughed and threw up his hands.

I didn't get much time with him after that. I thought I would catch him at lunch, but he was nowhere to be found, so I took my food to my spot under the tree. My lunch tray hit the ground and food spilled everywhere when I saw Tremaine sitting there, laughing, and holding hands with Vanessa. After I got another tray, I went to my car and scarfed down my lunch and sulked in private. Before I could clean my face, Carmen knocked on the front passenger window. "Mind if I join you?" she asked. I smiled and unlocked the door.

We reclined our seats, blocked out the sun, and listened to the radio until the bell rang for class. On our way back in, Tremaine saw us and ran to catch up. "What's up?" he asked. I had already made up my mind that I was going to give him the silent treatment, to see if he even cared, but when he smiled and stuck a piece of gum in his mouth, weakness filled every inch of my body and I caved.

"I see you found some new friends," I said. He looked back in time to catch Cody grinning and waving like a creep.

"Them?" he asked. "Nah. They just nosy. Wanted to know where I got my kicks from…If I had a girlfriend… stuff like that. Thought they was knock-offs," he said, laughing. Neither of us laughed with him so he made his way right in between us, wrapping his arms around our shoulders.

"Do you mind?" Carmen asked sternly while watching me. The corners of her mouth trembled as she struggled to keep from laughing in his face. We were doing a horrible job of pretending to be mad at him.

He turned to me, still smacking on his gum, breath smelling minty fresh, and pointed at Carmen. His head followed his finger as he asked, "Sup with her?"

"She can hear you," Carmen said loudly. Tremaine snatched a book from her hands and opened it. When a picture fell out of it, Carmen quickly picked it up before either of us could see it. Then, she took her book back from Tremaine. "Is this how you treat all your friends?" she asked. I giggled a little.

"Now you?" she asked.

"You have a little something on the corner of your mouth," Tremaine said.

When she reached up to wipe it, Tremaine grabbed the book back and took the picture out.

"What is it? Can I see it?" I asked while pulling on Tremaine's arm.

His face softened as he handed the picture and book back. "She died during freshman year. We never even got to meet in person," Carmen said, stuffing the picture back inside. Tremaine wrapped his arm around hers.

"I lost my grandma back in May, so I understand," he said.

We watched as she went and found a seat in class.

103

The bell rang and Tremaine and I looked at one another and rolled our eyes and went our separate ways for our electives.

On my way to Home Economics, I passed Brandy in the hallway, hanging up a poster for the senior's spring fashion show, while one of her gremlins, Fae, stuck them in the cracks of everyone's lockers. I grabbed a flyer from Fae and Brandy ripped it from my hands, giving me a papercut. "What the hell, Brandy?" I shouted.

She passed my flyer to another kid and gave Fae a nasty look. "No need to inquire. You have no sense of style and no one would dare try and dress that…body," she said. I knew she was still trying to hurt my feelings, so I didn't even bother to respond. I ripped another flyer from Fae's hands and stuffed it in my backpack, right in Brandy's face. She stomped her feet and pouted like a little kid.

"You dropped something," I told her.

She looked around the floor, even going as far as to pick her feet up. "I don't see anything," she hissed.

"Your bottom jaw is on the floor. You might wanna pick it up," I said.

She rolled her eyes, snatched the other flyers from Fae, and tried to storm off when the strap on one of her sandals broke and she fell into a locker. I was headed to class when I heard a loud BANG. When I turned around, I saw Brandy on the floor. Fae tried to help her up, but she shoved her. I couldn't help but laugh a little as Fae stood to the side trying to decide if she was brave enough to do the same.

We had a substitute in class that day, and the only assignment our teacher left for us was to watch a documentary on human reproduction. Half the class put their heads down and took naps, while the nerds on the front row were completely tuned in. Our substitute was too into fixing her hair in her compact mirror and polishing her engraved gold tooth to notice a few kids who had left for the restroom never returned.

I had developed quite the stomach when it came to watching babies come into the world. Once a year, Mama would sit me down and make me watch the same video and give me this speech about boys and babies. "Been there, done that," I mumbled to myself.

With nothing else to do, I decided to doodle. All my notebooks had been somewhat filled with my terrible stick figures, so I pulled the fashion show flyer from my bag. On the back, I filled it with some sketches of me on the set of a tv show, in front of a live studio audience.

I didn't know anyone who would take me seriously in the television industry. They would laugh me right out of my first audition. Ever since I watched *Boyz in the Hood*, I'd secretly rehearsed Nia Long's lines. I knew that if her rich almond skin colored skin was good enough for her to make it onto the big screen, mine was too. Although I was a shade darker than her, I knew it wasn't impossible. It would just be a little harder.

Some nights, before bed, I would make sure Mama and Chase were asleep before going back in the living room and turning our big screen on, lighting the place up, watching my favorite movies. I tried desperately to mimic her style, but I just could not get the crying on cue part down yet. I was close though. I could feel it.

I was too embarrassed to tell Mama that instead of going to college, I wanted to pursue acting. I knew Daddy would support me. But Mama always got the final say in anything I did, and they both believed in the power of a "good education". She had decided that I was going to get a degree and a good-paying job, so I could take care of both of them one day when they got old.

When class was over, I was trying to stuff the flyer back in my backpack when I got to the hallway and ran into Tremaine. "What's this?" he asked, pulling the flyer from my backpack.

"It's for Carmen. My mama bragged to me about how she had these big dreams of becoming a fashion designer," I said.

"That's nice of you."

"It's not a big deal."

"If you say so. You really need to lighten up and smile more. I promise it'll change your whole mood," he said, forcing the corners of my mouth to turn up.

He was right, but I would never let him know that. I was used to not having much to smile about but being able to help him and Carmen with even the smallest stuff made me feel better about myself. It felt good to have friends again after I had to leave all of my friends from freshman year behind. The thought of being out in the world alone again scared me more than anyone knew.

After school, Tremaine and I rode around and blasted my car stereo, doing donuts in the street when no one was looking. He almost flipped my car over when I let his long-legged behind drive. He mashed the gas too fast and we ended up on the curb, a few inches from someone's mailbox. Getting fussed at by Mama and Mama Joyce for picking Chase up late was worth it. Nothing could take my smile for the rest of that day.

CHAPTER 22

CARMEN

Living with the Butler family wasn't at all what I thought it would be like. I could feel the tension in the air every time I got ready for bed and even riding to and from school with Siobhan. I felt out of place. And while I wasn't worried about how I would eat or having the utilities cut off, I had a new set of problems. Between trying to keep Mami from dragging me to a shelter, and working with Ms. Shanté, who was uneasy about being around Mami, I felt like at some point, a conversation needed to happen.

Four women and a little boy in a three-bedroom house was a lot. At work, things had changed. Ms. Shanté and

I talked less and focused more on work. I appreciated her for letting us stay, but it felt weird being around her after the fire. Our dance breaks were our time to talk about any and everything on our minds...Things I could never go to Mami about.

Siobhan had her own life and already had a friend. And while I was trying to warm up to the idea of being her roommate, I think she was less focused on getting to know me and more concerned with how she looked and being in the friend zone with Tremaine, whom I could tell she was already crazy about.

When I started at Pulliam Prep, I didn't know what to expect. I was pleasantly surprised to see more kids who looked like me, who paid attention in class. I wasn't walking in on kids having sex in the girl's room, and the boys looked, but never touched. I could deal with an "aye, girl" or a "damn, baby" here and there, as long as they knew to keep their hands to themselves. At just five feet and two inches tall, I learned early on to show people that being short didn't mean I was going to be bullied or serve as a target for anybody's bull shit.

While I assumed that being the new girl at school would be an awkward time in my life, Siobhan and Tremaine kindly walked me to my homeroom, and every other class, making sure I was okay.

I couldn't tell who everybody was checking for when we walked together. Siobhan always had her long, milk chocolate covered legs exposed, and Tremaine was just bad in every sense of the word. He was unbelievably handsome. His smile could light up a room. And I'm almost certain he was the only boy in school who wore cologne. It even made me weak in the knees, to the point where I faked having to freshen up, to get away from the two of them, and get myself together.

My first week was okay. I had always done well in my previous schools, so I knew there was nothing here I couldn't handle. But somebody decided to put me into advanced placement classes and didn't tell me. By the end of the week, I had a backpack full of homework that wouldn't leave any time for sewing or designing after school. As if being new wasn't enough, everyday everybody just watched and waited to see who I would sit with at lunchtime. Every single time I would sit with Siobhan and Tremaine. If I tried not to, Tremaine would come to find me, like I was lost or something.

After about a week or two, Ms. Shanté suggested that Siobhan and I go to the homecoming game, to get out of the house. She gave each of us a few dollars to get in and for the concession stand. I was confused when Siobhan started packing up Chase's little backpack. "He's going too?" I asked.

In a very matter of a fact tone, she replied, "You got a problem with that?"

On the way to the game, Chase played with his toys in the backseat while I tried to pull myself together. Siobhan and I had our highs and our lows. Some days we would be cool, laughing together, having a great time. Other days she would have this nasty attitude like she wanted me out of her space. Trust me. If I had somewhere else to go, I would have been gone.

Luckily, the ride to the stadium was a short one. The Pulliam Prep Panthers were taking on the Sanchez Academy Bull Dogs. Before kickoff, Chase got a little fussy and Siobhan struggled to calm him down. One by one, people started to move away from us, but still managed to stare from a distance. As embarrassing as it was, I tried to tune it out and watch the game in peace. By halftime, Chase was fast asleep, and Siobhan and I started passing him back and forth after our arms would go numb. He was a little chunky thing, but he was so cute.

Once we were sure Chase was out for the count, we started cheering for our school, and saw Tremaine on the sidelines, chilling. He gave us a nod and turned back to the game like he didn't know us. Siobhan jumped up like she was his girlfriend and said, "I know he saw us!"

Just before half-time, I tried to beat the long lines and I went to get us some nachos and drinks. While at the concession stand, a group of girls walked up behind me, laughing and talking loud enough to where the band's version of "We Will Rock You" was a distant whisper. One of them "accidentally" bumped into me and wasted what was left of her drink on my Chuck Taylors. When I turned around, they were still giggling, until I pushed the troll who disrespected my kicks. "You can't do that!" one of them shrieked.

"Who's gonna stop me?" I asked. Neither of them responded.

We stood there and stared each other down until a worker called my order. "Two nachos with jalapenos and two sodas?"

I grabbed our order and stuffed our can sodas in my purse. As I walked off, one of the girls stood in my way, as if I was supposed to be intimidated by her. When she didn't move, I "accidentally" wasted my tray of nachos all over her. "Oops. Your bad," I said, walking off, as a smile escaped my lips.

"What took so long?" Siobhan asked as she stuffed her mouth. "Where's your food?" I pulled our drinks from my bag and handed her an orange soda. "Some putas tried to punk me," I said, looking over Siobhan's shoulder, giving the group of girls the stink eye.

"Girl, what did you do?" she asked, looking in the same direction. "You stood up to Brandy's girls? That's dope! Nobody ever stands up to them."

"Girl, you can't be letting no wannabes punk you. Whoever this Brandy chick is can see me too if she has a problem."

Cody scored the winning points as the team and crowd ran out onto the field like it was a championship game. "Is it like this at every game?" I asked.

Siobhan stood and threw Chase over her shoulder. "Girl, we have been on a losing streak for years. Never won a single game," she said, trying to clap without waking the baby. I joined in on the celebration and waited for Tremaine near the exit while Siobhan locked Chase in his seat.

When the crowd died down, girls were all over him. He saw me waving, standing up on the fence trying to get his attention, and went the other direction. "Tremaine!" I shouted. He said something to the girls and came my way. I climbed down off of the fence thinking he was gonna walk around it and leave with us. He towered over me as the team came out of the locker room, yelling his name. "I got other plans tonight. I'll catch y'all later," he said. I didn't waste another second trying to convince him to leave with us. It was clear that he had made up his mind. When I got back to the car, Siobhan looked worried.

"Where's Tremaine?" she asked.

"He said he has other plans, girl."

She tried to pretend she wasn't bothered but I could tell she was. It was like it took a minute for her to wrap her head around the fact that one, they won, and two, that he had other friends now. She didn't say much when we got back to the house. We got ready for bed and turned on the television.

I was about to doze off when Mami came in and whispered, "Psst, come here. I need to talk to you." She dried her hair with a big pink towel, with a huge smile on her face.

"Mami, what's goin' on? I'm sleepy!" I said. She finished, covered her arms and legs in lotion, threw her hair in a ponytail, then got to the point.

"So, they have room for us at the women and children's shelter downtown. We can stay for three months. We would get a room to ourselves, with a bathroom and everything!" she said, failing at sounding hopeful enough to convince me.

I guess I didn't respond the way she thought I should have so she instantly got upset. "What now, mija?" I took a deep breath and left my feelings on the sofa. "You can go, but I'm staying here," I started. I could see her veins pulsating in her neck, but I pushed through. "It's nice here. We have food, Mami. We have water. It's always hot. I go to a good school. Don't you want that for me?"

Mami wasn't feeling anything I had to say, so she didn't respond. She started unfolding her sheets to make the couch. I knew that was my cue to leave. When I woke up the next morning, she was gone. I had no way to reach her, and a part of me felt like she didn't want to be found. While I was eating breakfast, Ms. Shanté came into the kitchen. "You girls hurry up. I have a client coming over in a few minutes," she said. I sucked down my milk and proceeded to leave when she gently grabbed my arm. "Your mom left you a letter." She placed a neatly folded piece of paper in my hand, then pulled me close and hugged me tightly, then whispered in my ear, "I got you".

CHAPTER 23

SIOBHAN

I was not looking forward to homeroom or any of the classes I had with Tremaine. When the bell rang for Physics, I took my time. When I did finally arrive, all of the tables had been separated for lab, so I scanned the room for my name on a table. Mr. Leon loved mixing us up for group projects, which I hated with a passion. Somehow, I still ended up being paired with Tremaine and he was unusually happy. "Where you been?" he asked.

I sat my backpack down and started reading over the assignment without speaking to him. "Oh, so it's like that? You still mad about the game? I started putting the burners together and measuring everything.

"Work together!" Mr. Leon said, yelling over everyone's side conversations but looking right at Tremaine and me.

"Look, just focus. I don't need you bringing down my grade," I said.

"Excuse me?" he said, taking a step back.

"Ms. Butler?" Mr. Leon called out. I looked up through my dirty googles to see the counselor by the door, waiting for me. I had forgotten about my appointment. I grabbed my backpack and left Tremaine standing there with a twisted face, with my head held high. But once I made it into the hallway, my heart started racing.

"You did your homework?" Mrs. Hall asked as she held the door for me to enter her office. I held my breath, due to the old mildew and mothball smell all the students tried to keep quiet about. To my surprise, she had redecorated with a ton of elephants and changed her color scheme to red and white, and her office smelled like potpourri. I sat down, with my backpack in my lap, hoping she would carry the conversation so that I wouldn't be forced to lie.

"So, what'd you come up with?" she asked, as she popped a few orange Tic Tacs into the back of her mouth.

"I like what you did with the office," I said.

"Thanks. I just came crossed over as one of the newest members of Delta Sigma Theta Incorporated," she said.

"Delta?"

"It's a sorority. Something women join when they go to college. It's an honor to be a part of one. You build lifelong friendships and network with some of the greatest people you'll ever meet. In my personal opinion, you'd get the best experience at an HBCU. Speaking of which, have you researched any? You're running out of time."

I looked all around the office as she talked. Her accolades covered the walls. She had rubbed elbows with some amazing people. Mrs. Hall saw my face light up when I came across a picture of her and Nia Long. She got up and walked over and handed it to me. "I met her on the set of *Soul Food*. They messed around and let me be an extra in one of the scenes at Bird's shop. It was the most fun I had in years. But that's enough about me. What are your plans, Siobhan?"

As bad as I wanted to run away, I knew there was no way of getting out of the conversation. Everybody wanted me to go to college, yet, despite being an honor roll student since elementary, I hadn't received a single scholarship offer. I had managed to score a 27 on my ACT and didn't hear a peep from a single university.

Truth be told, I couldn't afford college on my own. Although daddy would try to help me pay for it, I knew he wasn't going to be able to cover it all. They helped me with Chase since he was born so that I could focus on graduating, and I couldn't bring myself to ask them to carry me through college too. I saw how Mama came home, upset, lacking the energy to even have a conversation with me over dinner. Sometimes I had to force her out of bed for work after she would miss her alarm.

Daddy had just gotten to where he could afford nice things. He went to college and majored in Journalism and nobody would hire him to work in a single newsroom. Instead, he took up working in construction and teaching English to immigrants at night while working on his new cell phone company. I respect and love my parents for all of the sacrifices they had made for me, but if that was what I had to look forward to, with a degree, I was going to have to pass.

"Are you even taking this seriously?" she asked.

"Mrs. Hall, I don't mean any disrespect, but I'm not like you. Getting a degree won't make me happy. And it sure as heck won't guarantee me a good job."

She moved her chair closer and leaned in to ask, "How do you know if you don't try?"

"I just know. I have the grades but I have no desire to do backflips and stay up all night studying the same stuff I've

119

been studying for the last four years, on top of trying to work and take care of my son."

Mrs. Hall's antennae went up when I mentioned Chase. I had completely forgotten that nobody knew I had a baby. "Your son?" she asked. The room got so quiet that I could hear the hands on the clock ticking. When the bell rang, I shot out of there with a quickness…so fast that I almost knocked Carmen down.

"Damn, girl. Where you gotta be, going that fast?" she asked.

I ignored her and kept walking until I was out of the building. Before I knew it, I was back at home. Mama Joyce and the babies were outside playing in the yard. As soon as we made eye contact, the look on her face let me know I needed to go see her before I made another move.

"It's the middle of the day. What you doin' back at that house? You know Shanté don't play that mess," she fussed.

"Mama Joyce, I had to get out of there. I slipped up and told my counselor about Chase. And…"

"Now you call yourself embarrassed," she interrupted.

"Yes ma'am. Mama was serious when she told me nobody's supposed to know. You don't know how people look at me when we're all out together. It's like they know he's mine."

"Chile, and what business is it of theirs to know if he is yours? You need to stop worrying about what think about you and the decisions you make in your life. You decided to have sex. You messed around and got pregnant. You could've gone about things differently, but you had parents who had your back through it all. Don't you ever part your lips to tell me or anybody else you're embarrassed to tell people you have a child. He didn't ask to be here, and he does not deserve to be denied," she said.

My eyes filled with tears as Chase walked up to me and wiped my face. I grabbed and hugged him as tight as I could. He pulled back and asked, "Mommy cry?" I laughed as I wiped away my tears because we had been working on teaching him to never call me Mommy outside of the house. I guess that was as much a sign as any that I needed to figure out how to deal with my emotions about my future and people knowing I was a teen mom.

"I'll take him for the rest of the day, Mama Joyce," I said.

She smiled then handed me his bag and his afternoon snack. When I was halfway across the street, Mama Joyce called out, "Nap time is in 15 minutes!"

We played until he fell asleep, then I went down right behind him. When I woke up, Carmen was coming through the door, panting, and sweating. "You left school early? What the hell?"

"I didn't plan to. I needed to be alone," I said wiping the sleep from my eyes. She made room for herself right in between me and Chase's little body.

"What's going on?" she asked.

"It's nothing. I'll be fine. Just gotta figure some things out on my own."

Carmen was about to walk away when I remembered something. I grabbed and opened my backpack. "Carmen, wait up!" I pulled the balled-up flyer from between my books and tried to smooth it out. "The posters around school got pulled down, so I figured you hadn't seen this yet." She nearly knocked me over when she grabbed me by my shoulders and shook me around, screaming.

"Do you know what this means?" she asked.

Chase woke up whining and climbed down off the couch reaching for me to pick him up. Carmen scooped him up and swung him around, dancing to the music in her head.

"If I win this thing, I get to go to college! Please be my model, Siobhan! Please, please, please, please?"

I knew nothing about modeling, but I figured it might be fun to shake things up a little. It was time to make a statement. I had been quiet for too long. I stood there like a dummy while she held different patterns up to my neck, with Chase at my ankles, dozing off. We were up until midnight playing in clothes. That was the first time I really saw her smile since her mom left, so I let her have her moment, and I did my best not to fall asleep on her.

CHAPTER 24

TREMAINE

After witnessing the football team lead the school to its first victory in years, and the four that followed, I had more friends than I ever had back home. I had gotten somewhat close to Cody and started sharing plays from when I was on the football team at my old high school. He took them back to the coach and I have to say, they executed them well. But shit got weird when his girl, Brandy, kept following me around. To make things worse, he followed her around like a sad puppy. I knew she was crazy when she followed me in the bathroom at school.

"Yo, can I help you, shorty?" I asked. She locked the

door behind herself and backed me into a corner.

"I see how you look at me, Tremaine. The whole school can see it. Just give me what I want, and I'll leave you alone," she said.

I tried to pry my way out of her arms and get outta there, but she had the strength of King Kong and I think she bruised one of my ribs. "I know Taekwondo. You don't want to do that," she said. I knew she was crazy then. She started unbuckling my belt and almost had my pants down when somebody banged on the door. She acted like she didn't even hear it and dropped to her knees. "Yo! What are you doing? You gonna get both of us in trouble," I whispered loudly.

"Brandy, let's go," Cody said through the door.

She climbed back up, using the sink to balance herself as she reapplied her lip gloss. "I'll go first," she said, turning back to me, licking her bottom lip. "You will be mine."

I checked my lil' man out and made sure I was straight before relieving myself in the closest urinal. Then, Cody came in and used the urinal right next to me, instead of one of the three stalls the school took the time to build for us. Out of the corner of my eye, I caught him looking over at my junk. "Yo, what is wrong with y'all?" I asked, while zipping my pants. I could feel him watching me as I left the bathroom.

125

After school, I tried to catch up to Siobhan in the parking lot to ride with her, and she was about to pull off when Brandy jumped in front of me.

"Where are you going? We were just getting started. My daddy's not home. Mama's going out with her girls tonight. It'll be just me and you," she said.

I looked around her and saw Siobhan pulling out of the driveway. "Damn!" I shouted. I brushed past Brandy and started walking. By the time I made it to Siobhan's I could see her through her bedroom window, settling in bed and turning her tv on. I knocked on the door a few times before she finally answered. Chase was right behind her, with his arms wrapped around her leg and a sucker hanging out of his mouth. "Want some company?" I asked. She gave me this look like she was annoyed that I was even there. When she didn't respond, I turned back around and started heading home.

"Come on," she shouted.

I tried to keep from smiling in her face because I really didn't want to go home. It was one of my only off days I had that week and I hadn't seen my girls in a while. I walked through the door and picked Chase up and pretended to body slam him on her bed, tipping over a bag of chips.

"Tremaine! You play too much!" Siobhan yelled.

"Yo, why you so irritated with me all of a sudden? I

did something to you?" I asked. Then, *Are You Afraid of the Dark?* came on and she got quiet. Ms. Butler and Carmen hadn't made it in from work yet, and I was kind of hoping she was planning to cook something. When I couldn't wait anymore, I got up and helped myself to the kitchen and Siobhan followed me.

"Can I help you with something?" she asked. I leaned against the cabinet and watched her pull out two frozen pizzas. I wasn't used to any girl being as tall as I was, and the fact that she was as tall as the refrigerator made it so that she really didn't have to ask me for help reaching for things, like my granny.

"You mind?" she fussed, as I pre-heated the oven and sat at the table, watching her wash the few dishes in the sink.

"Look, I'm sorry I blew y'all off after the game, aight?" She kept washing dishes and when she finally ran out of things to clean, she pulled up a seat to the table. "I can have other friends, Siobhan," I said.

"You call them friends?" she asked while laughing.

"Why you trippin'?" I asked. I could sense her getting irritation, so I moved my seat closer to hers and whispered in her ear. "You need to relax, baby girl. Stop making a big deal out of everything."

Our pizzas were just finishing when Ms. Butler and Carmen walked through the door. Neither one of them spoke

127

to us when they came in. Carmen went straight to the shower and Ms. Butler went to her room. Siobhan looked at me and I threw her the same look. I put my pizza on a paper plate and we bounced.

When we pulled up to my crib, she grabbed my hand. "I'm sorry. You deserve more friends than just me and Carmen. If you like them, you can hang out with them, but you don't have to diss us to make new friends."

"I feel ya," I replied. "Good night. Get home safely."

She looked like she expected a different response, so I purposely left her hanging. I didn't hear her drive off until I opened the door. As soon as I locked it, I felt Uncle Tony over my shoulders.

"We're going to have to talk about your curfew, and you being alone with that girl. You can't take care of no babies right now, man," he said.

"I know Unc. I know. We just friends. That's it. Can I go to my room now?" I asked. He stepped to the side and let me through.

Before bed, I pulled my journal out. Every night, before I closed my eyes, Unc challenged me to write about challenges from that day and how I was feeling. Since Mama and Granny died, I became real numb to any and everything, especially other people's feelings. I kept to myself for a while, until I started school.

When Travis went to jail, I knew I was on my own and I ain't have my big brother to protect me like I was used to, so I went into a shell and stayed there, 'til Uncle Tony forced me out of it. At one point, I had stopped going to school and ended up in juvie when I got caught on the block by a truancy officer.

Unc didn't play that shit. I did whatever he told me, and he took care of me. I appreciated him more than he knew. I did my best to stay out of trouble because I had enough problems already.

CHAPTER 25

CARMEN

Plaid? Stripes? Polka dots? "No, no, no!" I cried as I ripped through a pile of fabrics and patterns. I'd just been presented with the opportunity of a lifetime and there was no time for sleep.

Everyone was snoring, as I stayed up late to sketch the ideas in my head. I knew with my limited funds that I couldn't afford to go all out for this fashion show, so that meant I had to improvise. With Siobhan as my model, nobody would see us coming. That scholarship would be mine and I lived for the day I would get to watch Brandy cry like a baby as I accepted my award.

I pulled out the flyer to see how much time I had to pull this thing off, and my heart sank into the pit of my stomach. To sign up, I would have to present two prototypes on my model by the end of that week. That was in just two days. Between both jobs and school, I knew there was no way I could pull it off. All of my other designs were lost in the fire, and I was faced with missing this opportunity or starting from scratch. So, I talked to Ms. Shanté and let her know I would have quit, if there was any hope of me winning. Thankfully, she understood.

The next day, I caught Brandy in the hallway and hoped she would be understanding of my situation. But this was Brandy we were talking about. She was reposting the signs for the fashion show when I approached her. Her crew, who was standing right next to her, scowled at me like a pack of rabid dogs. She rolled her eyes at me, then grabbed her tape and other posters and proceeded to walk off. When I reached out to tap her shoulder, she jerked away.

"Get off of me!" she yelled, causing everybody to stop and stare.

"I need to talk to you," I said.

She did her best to look past me, but I stepped over right in her line of sight. "I need to sign up for the fashion show," I said.

"It's not that simple. You cannot just sign up. This

131

isn't just for a chance to win a scholarship. It's a fundraiser as well, and we can't have you stinking up our show, with those rags you pick out of the trash behind the Goodwill." I could feel my chest beginning to overheat and the fire that was about to spew from my mouth was a force to be reckoned with.

I felt a hand on my shoulder and turned around to see Siobhan in one of my Tommy dresses and some white high-top sneakers. Not only was it fall, but her outfit was all wrong. If she had bent over, the whole school would've saw her panties.

"I got this, Carmen," she said.

"Oh?" I replied as she stepped in front of me.

"Brandy, I'm just curious. How do you know where she gets her clothes? Oh, that's right. I do remember seeing that shirt in my mama's bag of clothes we sold at our last yard sale. And those shoes? Definitely Good Will," Siobhan said.

I hadn't seen her that embarrassed since her last day at Beachwood High. "Sign up is in Mrs. Hall's office. Better have your stuff together or you might as well not even waste your time," she said. My face lit up, but Siobhan's posture changed at the mention of Mrs. Hall's name.

"You're on your own on this one, girl. Bye!" she shouted as she galloped down the hall.

I searched for Mrs. Hall's office and sat outside

during my entire lunch period. I could hear her conference with another student, and I tried not to ear hustle, but when I heard something about a brother in prison, I had to know more. As the office secretary stepped out for the restroom, I moved closer to the door and pressed my ear up against it. Nothing. Not a peep.

Then the door opened, and I hit the floor. Tremaine stood over me, looking just as crazy as me. "Hey, Tremaine! I stuttered.

"Go grab your lunch before the bell rings, Mr. Johnson," Mrs. Hall said, coming out of her office behind him. He kept looking back at me until he disappeared around the corner. My heart almost stopped when Mrs. Hall grabbed my shoulder.

"Martinez, right?" she asked.

"Carmen," I added.

"Right, right. How can I help you, Ms. Martinez?"

I held the flyer up, turning on what I thought was my "pretty please" face. "The deadline is tomorrow", she said, as she locked her office door and headed toward the front of the building. "I can't make any special provisions for any student, Ms. Martinez. If you don't have your things together for your application by the deadline, I can't help you."

I stood there with my mouth on the floor as she met up with a few teachers and left through the front entrance. I knew that wasn't the end for me, because I never took no for an answer.

CHAPTER 26

SIOBHAN

For the next few home games, Carmen, Chase, Tremaine and I were there, front and center. Mama got us some airbrushed t-shirts made to support the team and we were the loudest ones out there every time. One night, on the way home from a game, we stopped at a corner store to get some snacks so we could stay up all night fitting me for the fashion show. I stayed in the car with Chase while Carmen ran inside.

On her way to the car, she ran into Brandy and Cody. I couldn't hear what they were saying but Brandy left upset. She dragged Cody back to her little white Beamer like a rag doll.

"Everything okay?" I asked. She was breathing heavily as she passed me my drink.

"Here! Now let's go," she snapped.

"Hey, whoa! You wake him up, you're putting him back to sleep. That's the rule," I said, waving my finger like a schoolteacher.

"My bad. She just pisses me off. I hate when people pretend to be something they're not," she said.

When we got to my room, she showered and changed while I watched tv. During a commercial break, I held a silky green blouse up to my chest and pretended to be an office secretary. "Your 10 o'clock appointment is waiting for you, sir…Sure, I can tell them to come back. Whatever you need. You're the boss," I said.

Carmen stood in the doorway laughing. "Yes, sir. Your 10 o'clock is waiting. Is there anything else you need, sir?" she asked, mocking me.

I threw her blouse back into the chest and went back to the bed. "Oh, come on. I know you're not upset. I was just joking," she laughed. I turned the volume on the tv up. Then, my anger got the best of me.

"I don't make fun of you for doing something you love. I don't even want to be in this dumb fashion show. I'm doing it for you, because I thought we were friends. Last time I checked, friends don't clown each other when they're doing something that makes them happy."

She sat down and sorted through her chest and new projects while I vented, not saying anything. She pulled out a pair of hot pink pants and put them on the table by the sewing machine. The silence was killing me, so I turned the tv off and stared at her until she couldn't ignore me anymore.

"So, what happened with you and Brandy? Why does she hate you so much? She doesn't even know you," I said. Carmen kept prepping the sewing machine like she didn't hear me. "Hello?"

She turned off the machine and climbed in bed next to me. "You really wanna know?" she asked. I grinned, sitting up on my knees. "Pinky promise you won't tell anybody," she said. She wrapped her right pinky around my left pinky, and we shook on it.

CHAPTER 27

CARMEN

Since Siobhan wasn't going to let this thing with me and Brandy go, I figured I'd kill the curiosity bug that plagued her, with her nosy self. I had never told anyone what happened at Chasity's house party. The rule was what happened at house parties, stayed at house parties, but each Monday, after every party, word would have already gotten around about who did what and with whom. Brandy, André, Quincy, Miguel, Chasity, and I were all playing Spin the Bottle. I didn't really want to because of how weird it would have been to have to kiss or do something far worse with somebody else with André in the room.

He knew I was a little on edge, so he convinced me to take a few shots of Tequila. Chasity's older brother, Mario, snuck us a couple of bottles of liquor for the party because he knew she was one of the most popular girls in school, and everybody had to talk about her party, for the sake of her reputation. I stopped at three shots, but everybody else kept going. When the Tequila bottle was empty, the game began. After a few rounds, some childish dares and kids going in a closet for three minutes, doing who knows what, it was Brandy's turn.

Everybody was laughing and slurring their words when one end of the bottle landed on Brandy and the other end landed on André. Everybody got super quiet, until André burst into laughter. Everybody started chanting, "Do it! Do it! Do it!" Brandy and I looked at each other nervously. Quincy shouted, "You have to kiss for at least 10 seconds. That's the rule!"

André acted like I wasn't even in the room. When he leaned in to kiss her, I got up and left. Before I got halfway down the sidewalk, Brandy was running up behind me. "Carmen, stop!" she yelled.

She followed me all the way home. Had we not already planned for her to sleep over, I would have called her dad to come get her, if our phone wasn't off. Shutting her out of my room didn't keep her from coming in, forcing me to listen to her.

"You know I wouldn't have kissed him if we weren't playing that dumb game. You're my best friend! I wouldn't do that to you," she pleaded.

"Yeah, but you did. And we're not friends. When you go home tomorrow, we're done."

I was still going in on her when she grabbed my face and kissed me. When I opened my eyes, Brandy's were still closed. She looked like she was into it, so I closed my eyes for two more seconds, then I pulled away. Two weeks later, she was dropped from Beachwood, and we never heard from her again, until now.

Siobhan was fighting her sleep tough and was about to fall back on her pillow when she popped up, fully alert. "So, Brandy's gay?" she asked loudly. "Wait, does that make you gay too?"

"Siobhan!" I shouted.

"Sorry, sorry," she said.

"I don't know if I like girls. I don't even know if she likes girls. That was my first experience," I said as I began to yawn.

Siobhan joined me and we crawled under the covers and passed out. For the first time in years, my chest didn't feel heavy. I could finally breathe again.

CHAPTER 28

SIOBHAN

Things with Carmen began to take a different turn after she opened up to me about Brandy. After that, she wanted to vent to me all the time. From the time we woke up until we closed our eyes at night, she was right there, in my ear fussing about her ex and her mom's boyfriend. "And girl, did I tell you?" is how almost every conversation started.

Now and then, she would get a, "Yeah. That's crazy," from me. And every time, she knew that my mind had begun to wander. When she was finally done talking about herself and how miserable her life was, she caught me off guard when she started salivating while talking about Tremaine.

"He is fine. Ooh, girl. I wish I could find me somebody like that," she would say.

"You think he's cute?" I asked.

She spit out a mouthful of chips while laughing hysterically at me. "Girl, he is sexy! But I don't want him. I see the way you look at him. And the way he looks at you? Please!"

I didn't think that I had made my feelings for him that obvious. And she "sees the way he looks at me"? I was dying to know what else she had observed, but I didn't want to seem desperate, so I played it off. "Girl, I don't know what you're on, but Tremaine and I are just friends," I said. I wanted to be out of the friend zone, and I knew it was only a matter of time before the opportunity would be gone, but I could never tell him nor anyone how I really felt.

"Girl, tell him, or I will," she said.

"And what if I did like him? What would I even say? He doesn't like girls like me."

"And how would you know? Have you asked him? And if you like him, hypothetically, then you should figure out a way to express that to him…Hypothetically, of course," she said.

I saw the way all of the girls threw themselves all over Tremaine, and the last thing I wanted to do was fall in line. We stopped seeing each other as much as we used to, so if there was ever a time to tell him I thought I liked him as more than friends, it was gone. Or so I thought.

A few days after talking to Carmen, I found a note in my locker. Didn't say who it was from or anything. Being the nervous wreck that I was, I waited until I was home alone, in my bedroom to open and read it. While I was unfolding it, I noticed the distinct scent on the paper and I knew before I even read it, it was from Tremaine. I started to feel lightheaded, so I put the paper to the side and laid across my bed.

After stalling for a while, I picked the letter back up and felt like my skin was covered in. I scratched until I was sure I had clawed my way through my skin. The reality hit me when the clock struck 4:55 p.m. I knew that Mama Joyce was going to be calling or knocking at any minute for me to get Chase, so I had to get it over with.

"Dear Siobhan," it started.

"I hope this doesn't ruin our friendship."

Before I could continue, there was a knock at the door. I stuck the letter in my panty drawer and ran to grab Chase. "The daycare closes at five. Not 5:15. Not 5:30. FIVE!" Mama Joyce fussed.

"Sorry. I just got caught up with a little schoolwork,"

"Mmm hmm," she said.

Back in my room, I through Chase a few graham

crackers to snack on, while I got back to the issue at hand.

"Here goes nothing," I mumbled to myself, pulling the letter back out.

"*Dear Siobhan,*

I hope this doesn't ruin our friendship. Carmen told me what you said. You know, about wanting to date and stuff. I like you a lot and I enjoy spending time with you. I'm just not looking for a girlfriend right now. I'm just trying to get through this year. I can't have any distractions right now. I hope this doesn't make stuff weird between us. I just wanted you to know that I know. I think you're beautiful and you deserve someone who has time for you. I still want to be friends, if that's still an option. If you need to talk to me, you know where I am.

One Love,

Tremaine"

I was indefinitely in the friend zone after reading that. I still had to see his face every day and be reminded of this painful rejection. But rather than let him see me sweat, I pretended it never happened, and hoped he would do the same.

CHAPTER 29

TREMAINE

I imagined Siobhan had read my letter, on a count of I hadn't seen or heard from her in a couple of days. Business was slow the day Carmen showed up. She walked around, wiping dust off of everything on the shelves, trying to hold in a cough she brought on herself. I knew she felt me watching her, as she pretended not to see me.

After a few minutes of lingering, she picked up an old piggy bank and sat it on the counter. "How much?" she asked. I politely turned it around and showed her the sticker on the back that read $5. "Five dollars? That's highway robbery!" she said, as I picked it up and took it right back to its place on the shelf. Uncle Tony came from the back and stood in the doorway, near his fish tank that held three little bubble-eyed goldfish.

"Can I help you with anything else? Anything at all?" I asked.

"Yeah. Actually, you can tell me why you played my girl like that. She really likes you. She's good looking. You're good looking. So, what's up?" she asked, punching me in my arm like she was one of the homies.

Unc was still standing near his office door, listening, when I turned around.

"Look, it's like I told Siobhan. She's great and all that. I'm just not looking for a girl right now. I got other stuff to worry about. And if you don't mind, I have work to get back to."

Carmen looked over my shoulder at Uncle Tony, waved and gave him a fake ass smile before rolling her eyes at me and storming out.

"What was that about?" he asked, while walking up on me with a damp rag.

"Nothing," I lied.

I reached for the rag before he was ready to let go.

146

When he wouldn't loosen his grip, I walked away. Then he grabbed my shoulder and stared me down. "I know, aight?," I said. He loosened his grip on my shoulder and the towel and walked away.

As I dusted the shelves, I replayed in my head what I thought Siobhan's reaction to my letter would've been. Somehow, some way, I managed to make myself feel guilty for lying about my feelings for somebody I really cared about. I knew it was too late to go back on my letter, and the damage was done. So, I just hoped everything would go back to normal from that point on and prayed nobody would bring it up.

At lunch the next day, none of us sat together. Siobhan was in her usual spot. I didn't even see Carmen. So, I grabbed a seat with some guys from the team. I watched her the whole time, as she ate her little baby carrots and a sandwich. It was a few minutes until the end of lunch, and I felt like I needed to say something. As I approached her, she started wrapping up her stuff and walked right past me. At that point, I didn't know if she was mad or embarrassed, but I knew I needed my friend back and I had to do something.

CHAPTER 30

CARMEN

I sat in the corner of Siobhan's room, hand-stitching this bangin' skirt for the fashion show, as Siobhan continued to ignore me. A *Wayans Brothers* marathon was on, and I knew she wasn't about to budge for the next seven hours. Her sulking about Tremaine not wanting to date her had reached an all-time low.

"You wanna try on some new designs I'm thinking about for the show?" I asked.

No response.

When the show finally went to commercial, I got up,

unplugged the tv, and shut the door. Chase was down for a nap, so I knew he wasn't waking up for at least another hour. Instead of throwing a fit and cursing me out, Siobhan just got out of bed, plugged the tv back in, and laid back down. Since she wouldn't budge, I got down on the floor right in front of her.

"You have to talk to me some time," I teased.

She sat up on her knees and looked right over me. I tried one more time to turn it off.

"What is wrong with you? You don't get tired of getting on my nerves? Ever since you got here, you have made things worse for me. Now, I can't even be around the only friend I've had in years. Do you have any idea how that feels? It's best you leave me alone before you piss me off," I said.

That was not the reaction I was expecting. To be honest, it did hurt my feelings to know she felt that way about me.

"I was just trying to help!"

"Go help somebody else. I don't need your damn help," she shouted.

When I heard Chase start whining, Siobhan got even more upset. I went to check on him and saw a shadow move past the window. Siobhan pushed me to the side and went and locked up in the room with Chase. I went to open the door and Tremaine just stood there. He had the nerve to show up.

"Siobhan here?" Tremaine asked.

He wasn't interested in anything I had to say, so he stood in the hallway trying to talk to her for a good 10 minutes, before giving up. I had never seen the two of them like that, and it was on me to fix it. Tremaine didn't even speak when he left. He didn't even grab anything to eat. I knew I had really messed up, again.

CHAPTER 31

SIOBHAN

Grocery shopping for Thanksgiving dinner was awkward because Mama and I hadn't spoken in a while. She was always busy with work and she seemed to enjoy Carmen's company much more than she ever enjoyed mine. They did everything together and Carmen would always brag about how easy it was to talk to *my* mama.

Things with us hadn't been the same since I came home with Chase. For a long time, I felt like she had never fully forgiven me or gotten past it. Every chance she got, she reminded me that he was mine and that once I graduated, that I would be on my own with him.

"Go over there to aisle four and grab me some flour, sugar, and that graham cracker pie crust. And make sure it ain't cracked," she said.

I was glad to be getting away from her, even if it was for a brief moment. I took my time grabbing everything on my list, and my mind went somewhere else when I grabbed some canned green beans and looked up and saw a big Thanksgiving banner hanging near the entrance. In the window under the sign, people had donated money to feed the homeless for the holidays, by purchasing a paper turkey and writing down one thing they were thankful for in the center.

I couldn't name one thing I was thankful for. Everything I had cost me something. Being thankful for a healthy baby boy meant being thankful for a parent who resented me and who couldn't wait I was no longer their problem. Being thankful for new friends meant being thankful that I had to share my personal space with someone I had just met a few months prior, while also being thankful for God placing a boy in my life who only saw me as a friend, while I developed real feelings for him.

Being thankful for being able to attend a good school meant being thankful for the shame I felt while walking the halls amongst students who had none of the problems I did ,and while secretly hiding the fact that I had a child.

"Ouch!" I shouted as Mama bumped the back of my feet with the cart.

"Girl, where is the stuff I sent you at? Nevermind. If you want something done right, you gotta do it yourself," she complained.

She snatched the list she had torn off for me and continued shopping while I sat outside on the bench by the door, watching people come and go, grabbing last-minute things for their holiday meals. I was used to the last-minute trips and long lines because Mama did this every year. But that year she was going all out for Mr. Tony like he was her man.

"Let's go," she said, walking past me toward the car.

I unloaded everything into the trunk while she sat there and ran through her checkbook. "One more stop," she said, exhaling. I rolled my eyes and played with Chase until he fell asleep. I was almost asleep with him until I noticed us pulling up into the driveway of a huge Beverly Hills mansion. Palm trees lined the streets while lemon trees lined the wrap around driveway.

Mama had the biggest smile on her face as she hopped out and headed for the front door. An older white lady met her halfway and handed her a white envelope.

I could tell she was upset about something because she was talking with her hands and the lady had taken a few steps back. Then, Mama turned around and came back to the car. She slammed the door so hard that she almost broke her window.

"What happened?" I asked.

"She said I stole her jewelry…shorted my check $200. She said it was that or call the damn police. She knows damn well I don't steal. I have worked for this damn family for years and now it's a problem?"

I could never understand why Mama continued working jobs that made her so angry. I thought payday was supposed to be a happy day, but each one just made her more upset than the last. I knew when she was angry like this, not to get in her way. So, when we got home, I put away the groceries and fed Chase. She didn't even come out of her room until it was time for her to start on the pies for Thanksgiving.

The delicious aromas of sweet potato pie, apple pie, and her famous pineapple upside-down cake flowed through the house as I laid in bed, happy to have a short break from school. Then, Carmen came in. My curfew was always nine o'clock, but Mama was weak when it came to homegirl. She came and went as she pleased. She walked through the door after ten and Mama said absolutely nothing. She came in throwing her stuff around the room like a madwoman.

"Girl, what is your problem? Stop throwing stuff

before you break something," I fussed.

"Girl, shut up and leave me alone!"

She continued to toss stuff around and when a shoe hit my tv, it was on. I pushed her into the wall. "Are you out of your damn mind?" I yelled as I stood over her. She just sat there, holding her head, breathing heavily until I turned around. Then, she jumped on my back and pulled my hair. "Get off of me!" I spun around several times, hoping she would loosen her grip and fall, but she held on tighter. The screaming and knocking into the walls finally got Mama's attention.

She put a hole in my wall when she burst into my room. "What the hell is wrong with y'all?" Tearing up my damn house! Y'all got money to fix anything around here?" she shouted, staring at me. As she turned her attention to Carmen, her mood changed. She was always taking her side! I couldn't stand to witness how she treated me anymore, so I grabbed my keys and left. I don't think she even noticed.

CHAPTER 32

TREMAINE

My first holiday without my granny was coming up in just a few hours, and Unc wouldn't leave my side. I didn't know what he thought I was gonna do, but it wasn't that deep. I missed her, and my mama, but nothing I could do would ever bring them back. I had waited on Travis to call me all day. After about six hours and no call, Unc took it upon himself to turn on a movie for us.

"*Boyz in the Hood* or *Crooklyn*?"

I shrugged my shoulders as he popped in the *Boyz in the Hood* tape and started rewinding it. Not a smart move for trying to get somebody to stop thinking about their problems.

Usually, the night before Thanksgiving, my granny would be up cooking so she could rest the next day and smile as we all ate like a bunch of greedy pigs. Folks from all around the neighborhood would come eat with us and hang around while we played Spades and Dominoes. It got so heated sometimes that Travis would have to start putting people out.

Nobody ever taught me how to play Spades, shoot dice or none of that. Travis always said, "It's a grown man's game". Like he wasn't just three years older than me.

Unc couldn't do more than mix up a few cans of tuna or bake a frozen pizza, so I knew if there was any hope of us having a good dinner, I was gonna have to make it. But it was like he knew what I was thinking because as soon as I was about to ask, Unc said, "We eatin' with the Butler's tomorrow. Make sure you wear something nice."

The movie was finally ready and somebody knocked at the door. Unc looked and me and I could tell he wasn't expecting anybody that time of night. Matter of fact, Unc never had visitors, beyond annoying ass Whitney. He grabbed a wooden stick from under the couch and slowly walked to the door, then turned back to me with his finger over his lips.

"Who is it?" he shouted.

"Siobhan!"

I jumped up from the couch as soon as I heard her

voice. "What you doin' out this time of night?" we asked. Unc could tell she had been crying, so he moved to the side and let her in. He gave me this look, like "get her out of here", but I already knew what was up.

"Unc, you mind if we step outside?"

"Make it quick."

I walked Siobhan outside and we sat at the top of the stairs as she scooted close to me and laid her head on my shoulder. I wrapped my arm around her and pulled her closer. It was really chilly that night, so I knew she was cold in her *Winnie the Pooh* pajamas. The wind was blowing, and the moon was shining its light right on us, like a scene from *Jason's Lyric*. I didn't think guys were supposed to get butterflies for girls, but I always got that feeling in my gut whenever she came around, especially when I smelled the strawberries and cream shampoo through her fresh braids.

"What's up? Why you cryin'? And why you out here driving around this late?"

She just kept crying, then moved her head to my lap and took a deep breath. "I don't think my mama loves me anymore," she said. I ran my fingers through her braids, massaging her scalp, with one hand, and tried to warm her up with the other.

"Nah, she love you. She just…she just might have a hard time showin' it. Look at me and Unc. He ain't neva had no son, but he doin' the best he can. I ain't even his kid. Ya feel me?"

"It's different with my mama though," she said.

She finally sat up and stuck her arms inside her shirt.

"We used to be like friends. Like, I could tell her anything. She used to talk to me about everything. When she found out I had done something and didn't come to her about it, she changed."

"Well, what you do?"

The conversation came to a standstill for a minute. Then, she got up, grabbed her keys and gave me a hug. "I'm sorry for barging in on you like this. Thanks for being a friend," she said.

"Wait, Siobhan. Hold up."

She turned around and stopped in the middle of the stairs. I ran down and gave her a hug. "Whatever it is, it'll be alright." She gave me this smile as a tear rolled down her cheek. I just pulled her close and buried her head in my chest and kissed the top of her head. "I got you," I said. She hugged me tighter and we stood there for a minute, 'til Uncle Tony came to the door.

"Wrap it up, son," he said.

We laughed as I helped her wipe away her tears. I watched as Unc closed the door, and when I turned around, she leaned in and kissed me then pulled away. I didn't even know how to respond. I was so used to hustlin', I hadn't even realized I had never been kissed before. I can't lie. It felt good, so I kissed her back. You know them butterflies I was talking about before? Yeah, they came back. I walked her to her car and watched her drive away, hoping she would turn around and come back, and never leave again.

I knew if Unc had his way, she would never come back. He went hard on me about girls, like I didn't have a brain of my own. I was prepared to hear a speech when I went back inside, but instead, he had started the movie without me. "Really, Unc?" I asked, laughing.

"Shhh!" he said and turned the tv up.

I just sat down like nothing happened. Through the corner of my eye, I saw him looking upside my head, smiling. I couldn't hold it in. A smile broke through on me too. I think he finally realized Siobhan wasn't going anywhere and he knew exactly why. I did too.

CHAPTER 33

CARMEN

I remembered all the stories Mami used to tell me about Abuela's cooking, and how they didn't celebrate American holidays, but she bragged about how Abuela used to make the best Sancocho, tamales, and Arepa. When Mami used to let me talk to her on the phone, she would give me all of her recipes that she never let Mami have. She said Mami was a terrible cook. Her food was edible, but she could never recreate Abuela's best dishes perfectly. We would laugh together on the phone as Mami burned the Arepas every time.

One day, she just gave up. Not just on cooking.

On life. Calls to and from Abuela stopped and it was left up to me to figure out how to pull off the recipes so that we always had something to eat.

So, when I saw Mami on a corner of a motel parking lot last night, I begged her to come back. We didn't have a home anymore, but I knew Ms. Shanté would let her stay. I cried and I begged, but she just pushed me away. "Get out of here!" she shouted as some guy in a big gold chain and a black jogging suit walked up.

I never told anyone that I was still looking for her because I was humiliated after she walked out on me. I was always mean to other people because I had been slowly dying inside, never once feeling like anybody understood what I had been going through. That night, I was fed up with fighting for a life I no longer felt like I deserved. If she wanted to live in the streets, I had to accept that and walk away.

"Carmen, come cut up the onion, please!" Ms. Shanté shouted through the bathroom door, as I wiped away my running mascara. I stared at myself in the mirror for nearly an hour, trying to see what was so wrong with me that Papi and Mami wouldn't fight for me.

"Coming!" I shouted back.

As I cut up the onion for the greens, I tried to think about things that made me happy, but that list was so small. "So, what all are we having?" I asked, as Siobhan walked in the kitchen and rolled her eyes at me as Ms. Shanté stuck a pan of cornbread into the oven. "I'm sorry about last night. I shouldn't have jumped on you. I was just upset," I said, as she started peeling the potatoes. She didn't even look at me.

"It's fine," she mumbled

The phone rang and Ms. Shanté left the kitchen. I stopped cutting onions to try and talk to Siobhan again. "Look, I'm sorry about whatever you're mad at me for. I can't take anybody else turning on me. I just want to have what you have," I said, trying to fight back the tears. She stopped peeling and threw her head back, closing her eyes.

"You already have more than I ever will. My mama loves you way more than she loves me. Ever since you came along, I can't do anything right in her eyes. So please, spare me the apology if it doesn't involve you leaving!"

Mami never took care of me the way Ms. Shanté had. With her, I didn't have to ask for anything at her house. She worked hard and I could tell she hated her work, but she got up every day to help me and take care of her kids. She even told me that Siobhan was the best friend she never had growing up, but Siobhan really disappointed her, forcing her to draw the line between being a mother and a friend.

I knew it wasn't my place to tell Siobhan, but I was curious to know what she did. After I finished cutting the onions, I noticed a smile stained on Siobhan's face. I could

163

tell she was thinking about Tremaine. The only thing I didn't know was why she would be smiling after everything that happened.

After we finished in the kitchen, we cleaned up the house, then sat around playing board games. Siobhan got so serious about Monopoly, that we had to put it away. She only had enough money for two properties, and nobody ever landed on them or had to pay her for anything. She couldn't stay out of jail and Ms. Shanté just kept taking all of her money.

When the turkey finished and it was time to eat, we set the table that Ms. Shanté had rented so that Mr. Tony and Tremaine could eat with us, in the living room. They had just walked through the door as I was grabbing silverware for everyone. Siobhan came from the kitchen with a pitcher of Kool-Aid and nearly spilled it when she saw Tremaine.

"Girl, move. This turkey is hot," Ms. Shanté shouted as she bumped Siobhan out of her path to the table.

She sat the pitcher down and tried not to seem excited to see Tremaine, but she failed miserably. Mr. Tony was watching both of them with this weird look on his face. We all knew it was odd that they didn't speak to nor acknowledge each other. I had made enough trouble, so I stayed out of it this time.

"Anyone want to volunteer to say grace?" Ms. Shanté

asked. Everyone looked around at each other, grinning.

"Alright, I guess I'll do it," she continued.

As everybody held hands, closed their eyes, and dropped their heads, there was a knock at the door. Everybody's heads popped back up and Ms. Shanté followed Mr. Tony closely as he went to answer. When they stepped to the side, I flew out of my chair and into Mami's arms. "Got room for one more?" she asked. I squeezed her thinning waist as tight as I could.

"I'm so happy you're back," I said.

CHAPTER 34

SIOBHAN

I was happy to see Carmen's mom walk through our front door. I had prayed for the last few months that she would come and take her home and I'd have my room and my life back. Having friends wasn't as big a deal as I thought it was. It was tough enough trying to figure out what was going on with Tremaine and seeing if he had feelings for me, but it became too much when Carmen started meddling in my business.

Having to sit across the table from him during Thanksgiving dinner was enough to make me want to puke. I knew we had just kissed the night before, but something still felt off to me. I needed to hear him say how he felt about me out loud, or that kiss was just that. A kiss.

"Smells good in here," Ms. Daya said, as she pulled up a chair near Chase, then went to the bathroom.

Mama cleared her throat loudly enough to get everyone's attention. "As soon as Daya washes up, we will say grace and dig in."

I looked around the room and took in all of the smells and decorations that Mama put her heart into, and my eyes landed right on Tremaine, who was looking at me. A smile escaped the corners of his mouth, then disappeared as the table shook. His uncle did a terrible job of trying to kick him under the table.

When Ms. Daya returned from the bathroom, everyone had already picked over their food a little. Mama pretended not to notice as she attempted to say grace again. Heads down, eyes closed, and our hands intertwined with each other's, we listened as Mama blessed our food.

Chase managed to turn his slice of turkey into a pile of wet mush while Carmen separated all of her food carefully. Tremaine's plate was nearly cleared in less than three minutes and Mr. Tony was gaining on him.

Mama sat back and ate slowly. When it was time for dessert, Tremaine helped me clear the table and grab the pies from the kitchen while Carmen and her mom caught up, and while Mama and Uncle Tony made eyes at each other.

"Everything was amazing," Tremaine said. "Reminds me of my granny's cooking."

I smiled and went to the kitchen for a few more paper plates and was headed to the living room when he grabbed my arm.

"About last night…"

"Don't mention it," I interrupted.

"Who wants pie? I asked, gleefully, as everyone's eyes grew at the sight of Mama's pies. Carmen moved closer to her mom, and Mama and Mr. Tony sat next to each other. Tremaine sat right next to me. He even cut me a slice of sweet potato pie, before he took the equivalent of three slices for himself.

"Thank you," I said nervously. He didn't respond, but instead picked up his red paper cup and tapped his plastic fork on the side of it.

"Sorry to interrupt, but I'd like to say something," he started. "First, I'd like to say thank you to Ms. Butler for preparing this delicious meal. It's nice of y'all to invite us over. For a second, I thought our dinner was about to be some burned, dry turkey and some store-bought stuffing. But this was the real deal, Ms. Butler."

Everyone laughed as Mr. Tony pretended to threaten Tremaine with a black eye.

"I'd also like to take a minute to do something I saw on a tv show one time. I want to go around the table and have everybody tell us what they're thankful for. I'll start," Tremaine said. I'm thankful for a second chance at a better life. Unc took me in when I was just a knucklehead out there in the streets, throwing my life away. When my granny died, I kind of lost my way, ya know? But I'm thankful for him stepping in and taking care of me like his own. I can never repay you, Unc. One more thing. I wanna say thank you for the friendship that I've had the chance to develop with Ms. Siobhan here, and Carmen. I hope y'all in this thang forever, cuz it's gonna be hard to get rid of me."

"Speaking of friendship," Mama started. "I'm thankful that my baby girl has found some good friends in Carmen and Tremaine, and I hope you guys have a long-lasting and healthy friendship. Just always be honest with each other."

Tremaine, Carmen, and I all looked around the table at one another, kind of confused as to what Mama meant by that last part. Then...

"I hope you all don't mind. I'd like to say something too," Ms. Daya said.

"Mami, no," Carmen whispered, trying to cover her mom's mouth.

"I want to piggyback off of Shanté's comment about

169

being honest with each other. Friendship is something you three shouldn't take for granted. Don't let anything or anyone come between you. And never leave your friends out in the cold," she said.

The whole being thankful conversation had turned into something else and I knew it wasn't going to end well. Mama was getting heated and there were too many knives lying around that table for things to carry on like this. "Why don't we change the subject?" I asked. Mama put her hand in my face and cut me off.

"Is there something you need to say to me, Daya?"

"Actually, there is something I've been needing to say to you for 18 years now."

"Let's hear it. You wanted the attention. You got it," Mama said, then scooted away from the table and put her hands in her lap, picking at her nails as Ms. Daya spoke.

"Why is it that you feel you're the right person to teach our kids about friendship and being honest with each other? You put me out of your house when I was seven months pregnant, in the middle of winter. I had nowhere to go! I ate out of the trash can for a month before a homeless shelter had space for me. Now, you tell me. What kind of friend does that to another friend?"

Mama's ability to control her anger was diminishing and my heart was pounding. "We're gonna go," Mr. Tony said. "This seems like something we have no business being a part of."

Mama stood up, stuck her hip out, and cut her eyes at Ms. Daya. When no one was looking, I removed all of the knives from the table and scooted my chair back. Mama did not back down from anyone, and she most certainly never backed down from a fight, and I could tell from the way she was standing that that's exactly where this was headed. Ms. Daya had this butt-whooping coming since she pushed Mama in the store that day.

"Mami, stop," Carmen pleaded.

"No, sweetie. It's okay. You wanna talk about it Daya? Let's talk about it. Let's talk about how I let you live with me and my husband for nearly your entire pregnancy with the agreement that you were going to be working so you could have your own place by the time Carmen came. Hell, we met at the food stamp office and for some reason, you couldn't stay out of there begging for a handout. I got out and worked for everything we had! You slept all day! You made no effort to find work. Nico tried to get you a job working with him and you were so ungrateful that you showed up late to the interview!" Mama shouted.

This whole thing had been blown way out of proportion and was treading on the line of embarrassment. Mr. Tony and Tremaine backed away from the table and stood to the side. I stayed right by Mama's side and Carmen stayed right at her mama's side. She started giving me a side-eye as our moms went back and forth. I didn't want to be in the middle of any of it. I had problems of my own. When a cup full of soda flew across the table, it was over. The peace was gone. Mama must've struck a nerve because Ms. Martinez came out of her shoes and tried her best to get to her. Mr. Tony pinned her against the wall as she shouted, spitting all in his face.

"That's not true and you know it! You let that piece of shit control your every move, and whatever he told you to do, you did it! I had your back when he knocked you into the wall, while you were pregnant. I'm the one who was by your side when you thought he sent you into early labor! That was me! And you know what you did to repay me? You kicked me out because he told you to. He didn't like the fact that I spoke up for us, and I wasn't scared of him. So, he told you I had to go, and you tucked your tail between your legs and put me out. Yeah, you didn't know I heard the whole conversation."

Ms. Daya finally pulled herself away from Mr. Tony's grasp, grabbed her shoes, and headed for the door. "Mami, no! Don't go!" Carmen cried. The tension in that room was so thick, you couldn't cut it with a chainsaw. Mama never told me my daddy ever put his hands on her. And I certainly never

172

knew my daddy was that vicious to women. I had never seen him so much as raise his voice at anyone.

Right after Carmen's mom left, she chased after her. Tremaine and Mr. Tony grabbed their jackets and left too. Mama stormed off to her room and slammed the door so hard that our family picture fell off of the wall in the hallway and broke. Chase had fallen asleep in his highchair, with pie crust at the corners of his mouth, and his innocence managed to remain intact throughout all of that nonsense. I cleaned him up and put him to bed and cleaned up everything by myself.

Things had finally calmed down and I was slowly falling asleep when Carmen came back in the door. She came and sat down right beside me on the couch and broke down just as the opening credits started rolling. I paused it and gave her time to get everything out of her system.

"You okay? You know that had nothing to do with us, right?" I said, hoping to make her feel better.

Carmen kept her face buried in her lap until I scooted closer and wrapped my arm around her. "Hey, it'll be alright. From here on out, we have to be there for each other. No meddling. No drama. Deal?" She didn't answer. Instead, she pressed her wet face up against the side of mine and sniffled in my ear as she received my hug. The thought of her snot getting on my neck freaked me out, but when you have a three-year-old, you learn to deal with some things.

She finally pulled away, cleaned her face with her shirt, and laid down on her end of the couch. I sat there for a bit, expecting her to say something. She just sat back up, grabbed the remote, and pushed play on the movie. We shared a blanket and fell asleep watching *Waiting to Exhale*.

CHAPTER 35

TREMAINE

"Tremaine, you got mail," Uncle Tony yelled from the kitchen.

I was right in the middle of leaving a voice message for Siobhan when he interrupted. It was either finish the message, hang up and call back, or just hang up. I just hung up. I guess I wasn't moving fast enough for Unc, so he came and threw the letter on my bed. "Your brother wrote you again. Probably asking for some more money," he said.

I knew my brother, and if he was asking for anything, he really needed it. I always put about $10 on his books, every time I got paid. It wasn't much, but it was the difference between him eating slop or a pack of noodles for dinner. I couldn't imagine not being able to brush my teeth or bath because I didn't have money. It was an accident that landed him in there, and he only had a few more years before he could make his own money. By then, I would be almost done with college and we could help each other out. He was all I had, aside from Uncle Tony.

"Don't send that boy no more of your money. You got a future to think about. He shouldn't have done what he did in the first place. That's why I always tell you to stay out them streets," Uncle Tony said.

I didn't even give him my energy. Yeah, Unc was a good man and I appreciated everything he did for me, taking me in and all, but he didn't know a thing about what happened that day. Wrong or right, that was my brother. He wasn't even in our lives to know how bad we struggled, trying to get Granny back and forth to the doctor, keeping food in the house, and trying to keep Mama from pawning everything we had for drugs.

She stole our only source of income, Travis's product, and he flipped out on her. He ain't mean to kill her. My whole life changed in the blink of an eye. I lost two of the most important people to me in one day. Yeah, Unc tried to help a little by getting me in counseling, but we never really talked about it. He didn't want to know what really happened.

If he did, he would have known that in every letter, just like the one he had just put on my bed, my bro was making sure I was straight in the head. Every now and then he would ask about the "Cali girls". He thought I could hook him up with anybody.

He didn't like asking me for money unless he absolutely needed it. It hurt his pride the last time Unc accepted a call from him and listened on the cordless phone as Travis told me about having to give some of his stuff away, so the other guys wouldn't hurt him. When we heard the phone hang up, Travis said he had to go.

Unc walked in my room while I was reading my letter from him, and just stood in the doorway.

"Trav said he's gettin' out on good behavior soon!" I shouted, like a kid on Christmas.

He just stood in my doorway with his arms folded and said, "Come on. I'm headed to the barbershop". But we didn't go back to Big Ronnie's shop. We went to some new shop close to the apartment. It seemed like every time I looked up, Unc was looking out of the window, watching his back.

"You good?" I asked, as he was getting his line. He ignored me and started flipping through the magazine on his lap.

On the way home, I could tell something was up.

"Unc, what's good? You been on edge all day." He parked and leaned against his window, avoiding eye contact.

"Look, that letter Travis sent is old. I held onto it because I didn't know how to tell you."

"Tell me what?" I asked.

"Your brother is already out. He did some kind of appeal with a new attorney and they let him out with probation for two years."

I didn't know whether to be mad or happy. My brother was free. But why he ain't called me yet? "You know where he's staying?" I asked. Uncle Tony dropped his head.

"Tremaine, you've been doing really good since you came out here. You've managed to stay out of trouble and you graduate in what, like six months? When you graduate and move out, you're free to do as you please. I know that's your brother and all, but I'm the only family y'all have left. So where do you think he went when they released him?"

"Did you ask?" I asked.

Unc got out and went upstairs and left me sitting there looking crazy. I had to clear my head, so I went for a walk. Somehow, I ended up on Siobhan's doorstep, but I couldn't bring myself to knock. I turned around and sat on the porch and tried to make sense of everything. Then, I heard Carmen and Siobhan giggling as the door opened. .

"Tremaine...Hey!" Siobahn said, looking like a deer caught in headlights.

"Looks like everybody made up after Thanksgiving, huh? Where y'all headed?" I asked.

"Actually, we were headed to the fabric store to get some more swatches. You know, for the fashion show. You want to model for me?" Carmen asked.

Siobhan kept looking away, like she didn't know what to say, so I helped her out. "You lookin' real pretty today, Siobhan." Carmen started grinning and looked back and forth between us.

"What's this? What's going on here? I feel like I missed out on something."

"Come on. My show comes on at seven. Tremaine, you want to ride with us? We can take you home after," Siobhan said.

"I actually would like that a lot. I'm not really feeling Unc right now. He trippin'.

Carmen hopped in the front seat, leaving me squished in the back with Chase's car seat. Siobhan kept watching me through the mirror. I didn't know why she was avoiding talking to me but still making eyes at me when no one was looking.

We didn't talk much at the store, but while Carmen was in her own little world, sorting through plaid and polka dot fabric, I pulled Siobhan to the side.

"So, what's up? Why you acting funny?

"I'm not acting funny. I'm just…confused."

"Confused about what?" I asked.

Carmen waltzed back over and twirled in a circle, draping a swatch of a yellow pattern over her chest and butt. "Matching men and women's swimwear? Right? I'm a genius!" she squealed, as she danced back to the other side of the store. Siobhan tried to walk away with her, but I grabbed her hand and pulled her toward me.

"Tremaine, look, you know I like you. But I was just in the heat of the moment when I kissed you. You and I both know your Uncle Tony would go crazy on you if he caught us seeing each other as anything more than friends," she said.

"Kiss? You two kissed?" Carmen screamed, actually loud enough for everybody in the store to hear her.

"Carmen! Oh my God! Hush!" Siobhan whispered.

"No! You kissed! Wait, was it a good kiss? Tremaine, can you kiss? Siobhan, can he kiss? Oh my God! This is too good! I knew you liked each other. I knew it! Tremaine and Siobhan sitting in a tree, K-I-S-S-I-N-G, first comes love, then comes marriage. Then comes…"

Siobhan interrupted Carmen and dragged her to the front counter. She mouthed to me, "sorry", as I stood by the door waiting for them to be done. They whispered and giggled as I pretended not to see or hear any of it. Girls are terrible at whispering.

When Siobhan dropped me off at home, she got out and walked to the stairs with me. I felt her hand glide down my arm as her fingers swooped in between mine. Our eyes met and she just smiled at me. "What's this all about? You was talkin' something totally different back at the store," I said.

She leaned in close to my ear and whispered, "Nobody has to know," kissed me again and walked away. I watched her walk to the other side of the car, where I caught Carmen giving me a crazy look. Then, she dragged a finger across her throat and grinned like a psycho. Girls are crazy, man.

CHAPTER 36

CARMEN

Ms. Shanté finally came around after the Thanksgiving blow up between her and Mami. She didn't try to explain much, but Siobhan and I took it as "staying in a child's place", something Mami and Ms. Shanté constantly reminded us to do when they felt we were getting "too big for our britches". I hadn't heard from Mami since that night and I began to accept that this was just how things would be from now on.

Ms. Shanté even gave us a few dollars to go Christmas shopping. I never had anybody to shop for, much less anyone to take me shopping, so Siobhan and I made a whole day of it. With only about $40 each, we mostly window shopped.

But I did see some fly Nike's that I had to have. They would have been banging with my new wind suit.

Things were going well until we saw Tremaine and some girl getting real cozy and stuff. "Let's go over there and say hi! That's your man, right?" I asked. Siobhan ignored me and kept walking like she didn't hear me or see him. I watched them as we walked away and when he finally noticed us, Siobhan was turning the corner inside of Dillard's. I waved at him to make sure he knew I saw them. Then, the girl turned around and rolled her eyes at me with some stank attitude.

That boy didn't know what he wanted. This other girl looked nothing like Siobhan, she had this chopped up cut that didn't even fit her face. She looked smoked out and her outfit was garbage. What did he see in her, that he didn't see in Siobhan?

I tried to catch up with Siobhan inside the store, but she had gone up to another level, like she was running from me. When I found her, she was sitting near the dressing rooms looking like she was about to cry. I grabbed a cute dress off of the rack behind one of those hanging mannequins and went in the dressing room and put on a show for her. From behind the curtain, I shouted, "I now present to you the fabulous spring collection from Carmen Valentina Martinez! And the crowd goes wild!" I strutted my stuff on the imaginary runway in a pair of heels that were too big. Then, I let my hair down out of the ponytail it was in as I got to the end to pose for the imaginary press and spectators.

I could see her starting to cheer up, so I went in for the kill. I went back to the dressing room, put on a bikini from the clearance rack with some clear platform heels, and wrapped a beach towel around my waist. "Yes, yes! I know. It's fabulous. Get your checkbooks, ladies, and gentlemen. You don't want to miss this highly anticipated, amazing wedgie proof bikini. It'll have the whole beach talking." When I got to the end, I ripped the towel from my waist and threw it down as the crowd that had slowly formed clapped and whistled. Siobhan joined in for a second until her smile faded.

Completely out of breath and barely standing, I looked over my shoulder to see you know who headed toward us. Before he could take another step, I was in his grill. "Nope. What do you want with her? Where's your other little girlfriend?" I asked, blocking his view of Siobhan every time he tried to get around me.

"Yo, chill. It ain't like that. And what's up with you all of a sudden? Don't you got ya own problems to be figuring out?"

He was about to hear it from me when I felt a hand grip my shoulder. "I got it, Carmen. Go get dressed so we can get out of here." I took my time cleaning up the mess I had made, while a dressing room attendant watched, with her mouth turned up. Soft-spoken Siobhan raised her voice and I thought my ears were deceiving me. "It was just a kiss, Tremaine. It's not that deep. It didn't mean anything. Go on back over there with whoever she is. Let's just do ourselves a favor and keep it strictly platonic from here on out. Okay?"

My girl! She put her foot down. He couldn't say anything. Just turned and left. By the time I came back from the dressing room, Siobhan was standing near the sitting area, waiting for me, fuming. "Let's go!" she said.

"Girl, it's not that serious. We haven't even bought anything yet," I pleaded.

She grabbed her keys and purse and looked right past me and said, "I'm leaving now, and if you want a ride, I suggest you come on". We had once again gained an audience who was waiting on me to lash out. Instead, I brushed right past her and left the store. I wasn't done shopping and that was the most fun I'd had in a long time. I was done dealing with her bratty ways.

I walked each floor of the mall until I had seen every

sale and every single thing I could that was out of my price range. I left with all $40 of my money and my heart on my sleeve. The last bus was leaving, and Ms. Shanté had just imposed a new curfew of 10 o'clock, so I had to get out of there or hear her mouth.

No sooner than I climbed aboard and paid my fare, did I see the one and only, Brandy Bonds right by the driver. I tried to act like I didn't see her and found a seat far in the back, covering my face as everybody else loaded onto the bus. Before the driver pulled off, she made her way to the back and sat right next to me.

"Is that the new winter collection from The Fragrance Store? You smell nice," she said.

I pushed her head away from my arm and scooted to my right a few inches, and she soon followed. "What do you want, Brandy?" She laughed as if something I said was funny. I pulled out my Walkman to try and drown out whatever nonsense she was about to start talking and she popped it open and took out my Selena cd.

"Selena, huh? So cliché! You don't listen to anything else? No Backstreet Boys, no N'Sync, no 98°, no LFO?" she laughed.

"It's not cliché to like culturally relevant music. You have your preferences and I have mine. Let's leave it at that."

"You know, Carmen, it's okay to be a little different and dabble into new things," she said, as she moved my hair behind my neck."

Just a few months ago, she didn't want me to touch her. Now, here she is, in my space, telling me all about trying new things. "Brandy let me ask you something. Do you like girls? Because you sure are pretty close to me. Like, all in my space," I said loudly, making sure the whole bus heard us. When everybody turned around, she gave them a fake smile until they went back to minding their own business.

"When you're ready to stop hiding who you really are, let me know. Until then, I can't do the fake shit. Move on now, before you miss your stop," I said, putting my headset on. She tried to keep her head held high as she pranced back to her seat behind the driver, where she watched me until she got off. Weirdo.

CHAPTER 37

SIOBHAN

After avoiding Tremaine's calls for the past few weeks, Mama tested my patience and insisted that I called to invite him and his uncle over for Christmas dinner. I lied to her for days, letting her believe they'd been invited but she found out for herself when she called a few days before Christmas break and Uncle Tony told her that they would be in Louisiana for Christmas. I didn't like conflict and I certainly wasn't ready to face Tremaine again. I could tell from our last encounter that he wanted to talk, and I wasn't trying to hear it.

You don't kiss me and then go shopping with another

girl for Christmas. Who was she and why didn't I know about her? We were supposed to be friends, but I guess that meant nothing to him.

I was relieved to hear that they wouldn't be coming by because I knew that meant less of a mess to clean up afterward. Last time, I got stuck cleaning up everything and I'd be damned if I let it happen again. Having more people in my life and in my personal space brought out a different side of me, one I didn't know if I liked.

After a disastrous trip to the mall, I managed to leave with absolutely no gifts for anyone, so I had to take Chase with me the next time. I let him pick out a cute little gift for himself. As for Mama, it was hard to buy a gift for a woman who never asked for anything but gave so much. I could never repay her for helping me raise and provide for Chase when his dad ran off. Forty dollars wasn't nearly enough to get her what she deserved, so I settled for the next best thing.

On Christmas morning, the gifts under the tree were scarce. Most of them were for Chase. I had about three and then there was my gift to Mama. I hadn't heard from Daddy since he gave me my car, but it wasn't unusual, except for the fact that he never skipped seeing me for Christmas. That was Daddy, though.

I watched with pride as Chase tore apart all of his gift boxes and immediately started playing with his Tonka truck.

Mama and I laughed as we watched him try repeatedly to ride it across the carpet in the living room. "Okay, ma. You're next. Let's see what you got," I said, as I danced around in my seat like I didn't already know what I had gotten her.

"Awww, baby! You didn't have to do that! I love it," she said.

She stared at the family picture of me, her and Chase until she began to cry. I replaced the frame on the one in the hallway and got the same picture put inside a keychain for her.

"Come here," she said, pulling me into her bosom. She stroked my messy hair as I enjoyed the feeling of being in my mother's arms again. It had been years since she last hugged me. Even longer since she last told me she loved me.

Things had been rough on us since I started high school, and with graduation coming up, I knew things were about to get tougher. But if I had learned anything at all from my mama, it was that I could always come back home, if I really needed to. But leaving was what was best for the both of us, because we definitely needed our own space.

Without me and Chase around, she had no one. No friends. No boyfriend or husband. Nothing. Honestly, I don't think I'd ever seen her take anyone seriously after she and Daddy divorced when I was five.

"Okay, you have to open yours," she said, bouncing

so hard that I nearly fell on the floor.

My first gift, a small box covered in snowman wrapping paper, was a check for $1,000. "Ma, is this for real?" I asked. She just smiled and passed me my next gift. I shredded the wrapping paper again and unboxed the Nokia 3310. "Ma! For real? You got me a cell phone? This is so live! Thank you, thank you, thank you!" I shouted, kissing her all over her face. She grabbed and squished my cheeks together and kissed me on each one. With one last peck to my forehead, she handed me one last box.

"Now, I know you didn't ask for this, but..."

I interrupted her sentence and freaked out! "Ma, you got me tickets to see a live recording of *The Wayans Brothers*?" Oh my God! "Marlon, baby, I'm coming!" I shouted, dancing around the living room. Chase joined in with his tiny little moves and later Mama. That was the best Christmas gift ever. Never in my wildest dreams did I ever think that I would get a chance to see my favorite show recorded live. I had to tell everyone I knew.

Then, it hit me. The only people I cared to tell were away for the whole break. I had to contain my excitement until they came back. A phone, money, and tickets to be a part of a live studio audience was everything I never even dreamed of. "Wait. Ma, why'd you give me $1,000? That's a lot of money," I said.

"You graduate in five months. Then, what? You haven't made any plans to go off to college, and you have a baby to see about. It's just something to get you started. Maybe you could start looking for an apartment? I don't know. Use it to buy your first living room set. Just use it wisely," she said.

My joy and excitement slowly came crashing down on me as I realized my 18th birthday was coming up soon. That was my last Christmas as a kid. How did that never once occur to me? Mama pulled me back into reality, and I could tell something was on her mind.

"Baby, I know you probably think I've been pretty hard on you since Chase was born but I had my reasons. I felt a huge amount of guilt when you told me you were pregnant. I felt like I had failed you as a mother because I was too busy making sure you had a friend. Don't get me wrong. You are still my best friend in the whole world, and not many moms can say that. But it hit me hard when you got pregnant because I couldn't understand why you wouldn't tell me you were having sex."

"Mama, it was my first time. I didn't know what I was doing. Some guy had finally paid attention to me for the first time in my life and it felt good. He said all the right things. Called me beautiful. Told me I would make a great girlfriend and all that. Then, when I told him I missed my period, he went crazy on me. I was just as scared as you. I didn't know what I was doing. I didn't know the first thing about becoming a mother. I was embarrassed and ashamed of what everyone would think. Why do you think I didn't tell Daddy until I was almost due?"

I could hear Mama's heart about to pound right out of her chest. I didn't know if it was nerves or guilt, but she was holding back something.

"I'm sorry for sending you to that group home with all of those other pregnant girls. You needed me and I wasn't there for you. And I know it may seem like I care more about Carmen than I care about you, but Daya has been a mess since I met her. I knew Carmen needed me way more when they showed up on our doorstep. Her mom left her, Siobhan," she said, as she began to cry again.

"Ma, you left me too. You left me to fend for myself for eight months. When I came home from the hospital, you acted like nothing even happened. I needed you then, and I need you now."

Usually, she couldn't stand to hear how she had *failed* me as a parent, but I think she finally realized that I was growing up and she had missed out on a good bit of my life over the last few years out of anger and resentment towards herself and me. We stood in the middle of the living room and hugged for a long time. She just held me and rocked back and forth humming the relaxing tune of "You Are My Sunshine". I could still hear her muffled cries as she buried her face into my neck. "I'm sorry," she whimpered.

CHAPTER 38

CREMAINE

I tried to call Siobhan for over two weeks, and she wouldn't pick up the phone. Unc wouldn't let me borrow his ride to go check on her. I needed to let her know what was up and give her the gift I got her, but she wouldn't even talk to me. I didn't want to leave for my trip back home without easing her mind first.

"Grab your coat and don't forget the toothpaste," Uncle Tony said.

I think he was more excited about this trip to Louisiana than I was. I was going to see my big bro for the first time since I was 12 years old. I was a big ball of nerves, and I think Unc was too, because he just kept talking about a bunch of random stuff. He asked me about five times if I had enough clothes and constantly reminded me of how early our flight was leaving. The last time I rode on an airplane didn't go over too well. I was sick the whole time.

I slept the entire flight and only woke up during landing because of the turbulence. Uncle Tony threw a fit as the stewardess was trying to calm him down. He elbowed me in my eye, trying to get out of his seat. I wanted to laugh so bad because he was always this big macho, tough guy. It was hard to watch though, because it never hit me that his fear of flying may have been the reason that he never came home to visit us. Not even for holidays.

Once the flight landed in Shreveport, he was the first person off the plane. I had to sprint through the airport to the baggage claim to find him. He was still shaking like a cold, wet dog. In no time, we were in a rental and headed to our hotel room. It wasn't the best, but I appreciated him for doing all of it. As he turned onto Hearne Avenue, he gave me this sly grin like he was up to something. "Southern Maid?" he asked.

"Nah. Maybe a little later when they're hot. We headed to see Trav right?" I asked.

Unc's grin faded when I asked about Trav, like that wasn't the reason for us coming down.

"You good, Unc? I ain't mean to irritate you or nothing".

He turned on the old street we all grew up on. Everything looked the same. All the little kids that used to run back and forth to the candy lady's house, were grown up. All my boys from the corner, James, Mon, and Jay, were missing from their usual posts. Then, Unc pulled up in the driveway of this super old house. Patches of grass peeked from a yard full of dirt where an old, run down box Chevy sat on four flats.

A big boned lady came down off the front porch with a huge smile on her face. "You made it! I hope the flight wasn't too bad. You know you never did like heights," she told Uncle Tony. She bypassed me and went straight to hugging and kissing him and whispered something in his ear.

"Hey, Ma. This is Shonda's youngest boy, Tremaine," he said.

"Oh, I know who that is. It's amazing what you did for him...for them. Ms. Ophelia had no business trying to take care of two growing boys. God rest her soul. How's life in LA, baby?"

I didn't even know how to respond because aside from going to school, work and hanging out with Siobhan and Carmen, I really didn't have a life. "It's cool," I lied. "Hey, y'all know where I can find my brother, Travis? Mouth full of gold…short and fat."

They both looked at me and sat down. I knew I was about to get a speech. "Tremaine," Unc said, rubbing his hands together. "Trav has been staying here, with my god-mom, Nadine. She took him in off my word that he was a good kid who made a bad mistake and ever since he got out, he's been nothing but trouble. This is the first I'm hearing of this, but she said he ain't been home for the past three days."

They looked like they expected this from him. Like he wasn't capable of getting out and doing better. He spent the last years of his childhood in jail. He didn't get to finish high school, so no college degree either. He don't even know what it's like to have a stable home. Now, he's supposed to get out of prison and just make something of himself to keep people off his back? He ain't have a chance to start with. The streets was all we knew growing up.

"He got a number?" I asked. "I know he'll come home if he knows I'm here.

They both looked concerned as Ms. Nadine dialed Trav's number for me and passed me her phone. I stepped out on the front porch, hoping he would answer and save me the humiliation of proving them right. "Dis ya boy, Travis. I'm busy right now. Call me back. Aight? One," his voicemail said.

"Yo, big bro. It's me, Tremaine. Call me back. I'm at

this lady's house. We lookin' for you. What's up? Hit me back."

Uncle Tony stepped out on the porch with me. I felt like he was waiting for a chance to say, "I told you so". He didn't have to though. It was all over his face.

"If you knew this was gonna happen, why you even bring me all the way out here like this? I could've spent my Christmas in my room, alone." He took the phone from me and passed it through the door to Ms. Nadine who passed him the keys to our rental.

"Come on. Let's go for a ride," he said.

Ms. Nadine stood on the porch and watched us as we drove away, like something about this whole situation was breaking her heart. We rode around the city, checking out Unc's old stomping grounds, and mine. We stopped at Griff's to grab a big, juicy burger and cruised the city until the sun went down. It felt so good to be home, but I was starting to miss my home in Cali, and Siobhan.

"How about them donuts now?" I asked.

We pulled up to Southern Maid and the parking lot was packed with cars. The line was out the door and almost into the parking lot, but we still got in line. Man, the people in this city made me smile. They just reminded me of where I came from and where I wanted to go. I wanted to make everybody proud and tell the whole world that a young cat from little ole Shreveport made something of himself. I must've been wearing my thoughts on my face, because some girl walked up to me and stood there for a minute before speaking.

"I saw you smiling at me. What's your name? I'm Nae Nae," she said, smiling.

"Tremaine. Nice to meet you."

"Where you live? You look like you come from Cedar Grove. Nah, Cooper Road. Yeah, that's it," she said, talking to herself.

"I'm from Los Angeles."

Unc nudged me to move up in the line while Nae Nae kept working herself up to ask for my number. Luckily, the line moved fast, and her order came up before ours. She wrote her number on a receipt and handed it to me as she headed for the door. "Call me some time, LA," she said, as she applied a tube of grape flavored lip gloss over her thin lips.

After the temperature dropped all the way into the 30's, Ms. Nadine lit all of the gas heaters all around the house. We sat around and played cards and drank hot chocolate, trying to kill time. I kept watching the clock and the door. Every time I felt the rumble of a car going down the street or saw lights shine through the living room windows, my heart started racing. Finally, when I was in the kitchen putting our dirty dishes in the sink, I heard the screen door slam. I didn't bother getting my hopes up, because I knew it was just another neighborhood friend of Ms. Nadine's.

My heart dropped into my stomach when I saw him standing there, in the flesh. My big brother, Travis Goucher, looking nothing like I remembered, except for the gold teeth. He had slimmed down, and his face was covered in tattoos. It was like he didn't even recognize me, because he just stood there for a long time. "Give your brother a hug, baby," Ms. Nadine told Travis.

I tried to speak but my tongue was stuck to the roof of my mouth. He walked up to me and grabbed me, tightening his grip around my back. I kept hearing him breathe heavily, like he was trying to catch his breath, and when I tried to pull away, he gripped my shirt so I couldn't move. "I missed you, man," he said.

Then, we both just started crying. "Hey now. Stop all that crying. He's here now. Y'all go in the back and catch up some. Y'all got another day with each other. Make the most of it," Ms. Nadine said.

Before we went to the back of the house, Trav turned back to Uncle Tony and Ms. Nadine, cleaning snot and tears from his face with his shirt and said "Thank y'all, man".

CHAPTER 39

CARMEN

Mami and I hadn't been able to watch our Telenovela's since the cable got cut off last year. We were having the best time catching up and gossiping about our favorite characters, but something was different about Mami. She was finally smiling, and it didn't look like she was hurting anymore. "Mami, you look happy," I said. She popped a handful of popcorn into her mouth and kept watching tv.

"Mami, did you hear me?"

"Yes, mija. What do you want me to say? I'm happy! Gabriel makes me happy!"

Still not looking at me, she shoved more snacks into

her mouth. "When are you coming back for me?" I asked. "I thought this was temporary. I want my room back. I want you back."

"God, Carmen. Don't start. We were having such a good time. I thought you loved being over there with your *new* mami. She takes care of you and buys you nice things, huh? That's what you wrote in your letter, right? She buys all the food you love, and she cooks? If she's so great, why do you want to come back and live with me?

I guess the fact that she's my mother wasn't enough for her to understand why I wanted to come home, wherever that was. She chewed me out for asking for what I felt I should've been entitled to. I wasn't interested in our show after that. My attention had turned to the setup of the apartment. It was clean. Like, spotless. Cleaner than any of our apartments had ever been. Everything was in order, and I could smell bleach and Pine Sol when I walked through the front door. But as soon as I sat down on the couch beside her, I caught a strong whiff of weed, and a light stench of rotting meat.

"Where's the bathroom?" I asked. She stuck her arm out across my face and pointed to the hall toward the small, dingy hallway. Before I got to the bathroom, I came across a

203

room with a locked door. I looked back over my shoulder and she was still snacking and laughing. I pulled one of my pins from my head and popped the door open, quietly. Two long tables sat along the walls to my right, and directly in front of me was a huge trunk. I walked slowly, as I scanned the room and saw another trunk in the adjacent corner. There was a combination lock on each one and just as I knelt to open the first trunk, Mami snatched me up by my shirt.

"What the hell are you doing? You forgot what a bathroom looks like now? Down the hall to the left. And don't ever come in here again. You hear me?"

She grabbed my arm and dragged me to the bathroom and pushed me inside. Then, I heard the door to the other room slam and Mami mumbled something under her breath. Rather than pretend to use the toilet, I just grabbed my coat from the sofa and walked out. "Where you think you going?" she asked, as I kept walking. When I got to the sidewalk by the street, I looked back and the door to the apartment was closed. She didn't come after me... *She really didn't come after me.*

CHAPTER 40

SIOBHAN

"Suck it in for a second, girl," Carmen hissed, as we struggled to squeeze me into a lime green one-piece with black triangles all over

"Are you sure this is going to fit by the show? We only have two months," I said.

As she measured my hips and boobs, I watched over her head as every stretchmark around my inner thighs bulged from the stiff threading at my bikini line "Ouch!" I shouted. Loosen this thing so I can breathe! You want me passing out on the runway?"

"Don't be such a baby. You'll be fine. Now, walk to the door and back, like you mean it…and smile!" she said.

I started at the door, then the floor between my bed and dresser turned into my catwalk. I felt my butt cheeks crash into one another as my ankles wobbled and my toes slid forward, through the opening of the heels I was wearing, onto the carpet. When I got to the end of the runway and struck a pose, the whole left side of the swimsuit split open. I busted the other side as I fell out in the middle of my bed laughing. Carmen and I were cackling like a bunch of hyenas when Tremaine barged in.

"Tremaine, get out of here!" we yelled, tossing pillows and stuffed animals at the door.

"Put some clothes on, girl. And stop leaving the front door unlocked," he said, laughing.

Carmen helped me out of the swimsuit, and I threw on a pair of cartoon pajamas, hoping to regain my dignity before letting Tremaine back in. "Why in the world are you trying on a swimsuit in January?" he asked.

"Oh, don't worry. I got something for you too!" Carmen laughed, pulling a pair of yellow and black men's swimming trunks from her stash. We sat on the bed and nervously awaited Tremaine's return from the bathroom. Carmen opened up my swimsuit and added some extra fabric as I watched the tv guide roll over a couple of times, trying to decide between *Cousin Skeeter* and *Smart Guy* reruns. The laughter picked back up when Tremaine came in, strutting his stuff, with his tattoos and ashy chicken legs exposed, with no shame.

Carmen laughed until she couldn't stop coughing to catch her breath. When Tremaine walked across the room, I couldn't help but notice a couple of scars on his back and the back of one of his legs. The uneasiness I was feeling was hard to hide when he turned back to me with the biggest grin on his face. "You aight?" he asked.

The floor rumbled underneath us as Mama's headlights pierced my blinds and curtains. Tremaine shot out of my room while Carmen and I played it cool. At the sound of Mama's voice, fussing about the arrangement of the pillows on the couch, Chase woke up whining.

"Ma, come on! He just went to sleep!" I shouted.

She swung open the door to my room, just as Tremaine was coming out of the bathroom, fully dressed.

"Don't sit in my living room if you can't fix my pillows back how they go." Tremaine looked like he'd seen a ghost until Mama retreated to her room. Chase's cries faded out and he fell back asleep as things calmed down.

"So, how was Christmas? Anything exciting happen?" Tremaine asked, like he was about to burst with excitement to tell us something.

"Same stuff, different day," Carmen mumbled, packing her rags back into her box, trying to force it closed.

"Did I say something wrong?" Tremaine asked, looking at me.

Carmen finished putting her sewing kit away and left the room.

"What's wrong with her?" he asked.

"Her mom. Some things just never change, ya know? She didn't even get her anything for Christmas."

When Carmen returned, she changed the tv and threw herself across my bed and proceeded to munch on a family sized bag of Doritos. "You know Mama said don't eat from the bag. We have paper towels," I fussed. She just rolled her eyes and kept crunching. Dealing with her could be so exhausting sometimes.

"So, what did you get into in Louisiana?"

Tremaine smiled from ear to ear.

"I saw my big bro, Trav. We spent all of Christmas day together. Didn't even know he was out. Something about good behavior. I'm just happy he's home and clean. I think he's gonna make something of himself one day. I can't wait to graduate, so I can go live with him and go to school there."

"Wait, you're not going to college here? Why?" I shrieked as if he had just told me the world was ending.

"Unc said he's only paying for me to go to one of them HBCU's. The only one I know of is Grambling State University, which just so happens to be about an hour from home. I call that a win. Right?"

I didn't know if it was the news that he was planning to leave or the gut-punch of knowing we could never be together, even if I made a move on him that day. High school would be over in less than five months, and with the fashion show and prom just around the corner, I had it made up in my mind that there was no hope for us.

"So, what you get for Christmas?" he asked.

"I'm going to see a live taping of *The Wayans Brothers*. I got a phone, and…"

"Wait, got you a phone? Dang!" Tremaine interrupted.

"And some money…basically when I move," I said.

"Dang. So, she's counting down the days, huh? That's messed up. Why does she want you gone so bad?"

Scared of Mama overhearing us, I ignored the question and started opening my new phone. "You know how to set this thing up?" I asked, handing it to Tremaine. Carmen's smacking got louder as she laughed super dramatically at Pinky and the Brain.

"Girl!" I shouted.

"My bad!" she hissed, turning up the corner of her mouth with artificial cheese dust all around it.

"Here you go," Tremaine said, handing me my phone as it began to light up.

"Now what do I do with it?"

"You call people, girl," Tremaine said, laughing.

"I don't even have anyone to call," I said.

"You can call me. I mean, that's if you want to."

"Tremaine, you're always here. Like...always," I laughed.

We stared at one another for a second before Chase walked into the room, rubbing his eyes. "I pee," he moaned while yawning and trying to climb up in my bed.

"Oh, no. You come on here," I said, picking him up and holding him at arm's length from me.

I filled the sink with warm, soapy water and rushed to wipe Chase down so that he wouldn't wake all the way up and have to be rocked back to sleep. I was stuffing his head into a clean set of Reptar pajamas when I felt a presence behind me. "Yo, you a good big sister. I couldn't imagine my mom's having another kid with me almost out of school. He's gonna appreciate all this when he gets older," Tremaine said, as he leaned in the doorway and watched me spread baby powder on Chase's little chest and sneak a kiss in on his pouty little lips.

"I'm out of here. I'll walk. See you guys later," he said, still leaning and staring. After a couple of minutes, he finally walked away.

I put Chase in his bed, turned on his baby boombox, and ran for the door. Tremaine was nearly out of sight when I shouted "Hey!" He turned back and waved and kept walking. I went back inside, grabbed my cell phone, and sat in the dark living room, watching the clock. When 9:10 pm rolled around, I took a deep breath and did it. I called him.

"Hello?" Uncle Tony answered.

I nearly broke my phone trying to hang up. When it rang again, I felt sick to my stomach and just stood there. Carmen stormed down the hall and answered for me. "Hello?" she hissed. She rolled her eyes, then handed it to me.

"It's Tremaine," she said.

CHAPTER 41

TREMAINE

What are your long-term goals? What are your short-term goals? Why do you want to attend our college? What can you do to ensure that your time at our university is productive and equates to a fulfilling career?

If I had any hope of getting into college, I had to be able to answer every single one of these questions for my counselor. College essays were a requirement at every school she recommended. And every school she recommended just so happened to cost more than Uncle Tony made in a year, and none of them were HBCU's.

"If you want a real chance at getting into a great program, you have to consider schools with a great track record. College isn't all about partying. Yes, you want to have a great time, but don't forget why you're there. Now, the last time we spoke, you were telling me about your uncle wanting to send you to an HBCU. Any particular ones in mind?" Mrs. Hall asked.

I picked up one of the brochures in the lineup on her desk and slid it over to her. "You think I can get in here?" I knew USC wasn't on Unc's list, and it was definitely out of the budget, but I had to have a backup plan. Mrs. Hall taught me that. Plan A doesn't always work, and a Plan B is better than no plan at all.

"They have a very rigorous admissions process. You'd have to write an essay and interview. By the way, have you taken the ACT?"

If I had known getting into college was like getting a job, I would've taken Unc up on his offer for that management position at his store.

"Interview?" I asked. "And an essay about what?"

I could see the frustration in her face as she put the brochure back on the table.

"Look, Tremaine. I don't want you to feel like I'm rushing you, but this is your last semester of high school. This is it. School's like USC are no joke. I'm not doubting you'd be able to test and interview well. There's an ACT coming up in a few weeks, and I could work with you to help you get ready for the interview, but…"

"Let's do it," I said, standing and throwing my backpack on my back.

Mrs. Hall stood and stuck out her hand. "You can do this," she said, smiling. "I'm so proud of you. I'm rooting for you."

I knew Unc had his heart set on me going to a certain school, even if it was all the way back in the south, where he definitely didn't want me spending any additional time, but something in me felt like I owed it to myself, my granny and Uncle Tony, to make the best decision possible for my future. Grambling had been a part of the plan since just before my granny died. Everybody talked about going there and I knew I wouldn't feel so alone if I went back to my comfort zone. I looked forward to the homecoming games, the parties on the yard, having a roommate from some random part of the country, and getting to go home to Granny's to wash my clothes on the weekend to eat a good, hot meal.

Part of me still wanted all of that. The only thing missing was my granny, and I just knew things wouldn't be the same without her there. Yeah, I had Trav, but Unc said it was only a matter of time before he went back to jail. Before we even left after Christmas, word got out that him and a couple of his homies broke into somebody's house and stole some weed. I didn't need that kind of heat on me in school, so I knew I had to think long and hard about this decision.

When I got to work, Unc wasn't there. Hubert, the new guy that Unc hired off the street, was walking around the shop with his chest stuck out, like he ran the place. It was almost closing time when Uncle Tony finally came through the door. He was panicked and out of breath, trying to play like everything was cool. He couldn't even stand up straight, much less walk without stumbling. Me and Hubert helped him to the back, and I went back out front and turned off the open sign and locked up. I was putting the VCR's and camcorders up when some dude came and knocked on the door.

"Yo, I need to pawn this chain real quick," he shouted, spitting on the glass.

"Hey man, we're closed. Come back tomorrow," I said.

He didn't take no for an answer and started beating on the door again.

"Let me in man. Please!"

After a stare down of about 15 seconds, he looked back over his shoulder and ran. I hid in the back with Unc and Hubert for a few more minutes until we felt it was safe to leave. I wanted to ask Unc what was going on, but every time

I looked concerned and even acted like I was about to ask, he said, "Leave it alone".

He was propped up against my backpack and I saw my application for USC, and some other local colleges hanging out. Hubert left first, while we pulled the gate down and headed to the car. Out of nowhere, Unc threw me down on the concrete as a glass bottle smashed against the gate, and fell on me, cutting my arm. I heard a car burning rubber and speeding away as Unc tore off a piece of his t-shirt and tied it around my arm. We ran to the car and pushed about 50 trying to get home.

When we got to the apartment, Uncle Tony power-walked from room to room, grabbing pillows and blankets, throwing them on the floor, between the couch and loveseat. He pulled his gun from under a shelf in his entertainment system and put it on the coffee table next to his pallet. We shut off all the lights and got down on the floor. I could hear his heart beating from four feet away. Not knowing how long it would be before we both fell asleep, I ran to my room and grabbed my journal and dashed back to the living room.

Just under a year ago, my granny took her last breath, right beside me, asleep in her favorite recliner. I sat near the front door, holding a pack of frozen peas up to my right eye when they came knocking. With my vision blurred, I struggled to focus on the space between granny's burgundy curtains and dusty blinds. I saw somebody run down off the porch and hop into a '67 Cutlass.

About ten minutes later, I called 9-1-1. When the ambulance finally showed up, they worked on my granny for a few minutes before I heard, "I got a faint pulse. What hospital would you like for us to take her to?" One of the EMT's asked.

I remembered all too well how this situation could have ended. Somebody was after me the night I lost my Granny to a heart attack. They tried everything they could to get in our house, but the police and ambulance showed up as soon as they broke a back window. I crouched down on the floor on the side of her recliner, praying, asking God for another chance to do things right. I never knew fear like that again until the night I saw Unc cowering in his own crib.

He didn't have to tell me, because I knew he was in some kind of trouble. He had been taking money straight out of the register at closing and that was about the only time we saw him during store hours, for close to a week. I knew homeboy that was tryna get in after we closed was after Unc. I just thought it was funny how he lectured me about being in the streets, and he still was. I was about to ask the obvious, when a shadow moved near the window at the top of the front door.

"Antonio, I know you in there! Bring yo scary ass out here. And you better have my money," Big Ronnie yelled.

Sweat was pouring from Uncle Tony's head as he tried to call the police. His hands were shaking so bad that he could only dial the nine.

"What money is he talking about, Unc?"

He ignored me and kept trying to dial 9-1-1. I kept watching the door and saw the shadow leave.

"I think he's gone," I whispered.

We slept on the living room floor that night. I ain't like having to watch my back, and I wasn't about to let Unc get me caught up in his mess, so the next day, I gave him some of the money Travis gave me for Christmas. He hesitated about taking it at first, but when a car drove past the store and backfired, he grabbed the money, went to the back and locked himself in his office for the rest of the day.

CARMEN

CHAPTER 42

Everything that I had worked so hard for had come full circle
for me. The judges for the fashion show had been
announced, and I was a nervous wreck. Kimora Lee
Simmons, the editor-in-chief of Jet Magazine and Alicia
Silverstone from *Clueless* were going to be judging my designs
and choosing me as the winner of our fashion show. I knew
I had to come with my A-game to take this one home, with
only a few weeks left until showtime, I cut out all distractions
and went to work.

Siobhan's room was a mess. I had to pull out all of
my designs and do a quick run-through with her to see if I
was sure about my spring line.

The one thing I hadn't figured out yet was a name for my brand. Nothing sounded good or catchy. None of the ideas I had written down were making sense, so I tossed them on the floor and started over more times than I could count. Nothing was clicking with me until Siobhan walked in and took the scraps of ideas I had balled up to throw away and put them together like a puzzle. She sat on the floor and looked at them for a while before she said anything.

"What about Bella Valentina?" she asked.

It did have a ring to it. "Bella Valentina? I like that," I said. The more I said it out loud, the more legit it sounded. It was then that everything began to flow and come together. My orange, yellow, and lime green spring line, was going to be a hit. The yellow and orange pieces looked great against Tremaine and Siobhan's brown skin, and the lime green just added a special kick and brought each piece together.

I grinned as I imagined the whole school chanting my name as we awaited the announcement of the winner of the show. Getting my designs in front of THE Kimora Lee Simmons was big, and I knew if I wanted her to take me seriously, I had to go hard. The people from JET magazine were looking to add to their beauty section by including up and coming designers. Imagine my name in a magazine. Bella Valentina is going to be the talk of the town.

I got so carried away with daydreaming that I hadn't realized prom was a month away. Nobody had even said anything. Siobhan had moved on and was glued to the tv, without a care in the world. While I carefully looked over my pieces to make a note of alterations that needed to be done, I started thinking of what scraps would look good stitched together to make a badass gown.

"Hey, are we going to prom together?" I asked.

"Prom? You really want to go? Shouldn't we have dates for that?" Siobhan asked.

I sat my things down and joined her on the bed.

"I mean, we don't have to. We could be each other's date. You think Tremaine would want to go with us?"

"I think he's going to ask somebody else. He hasn't said anything about it though."

When her show came back on, a lightbulb went off in my head. "Hey, why don't we all dress alike? We could all rock some Bella Valentina originals. I'm sure your mom would appreciate not having to spend money on a dress for you to wear one time."

"You don't have time for that. You need to focus on winning this scholarship so you can go to college, blow up and I can come live with you. Prom isn't that big of a deal," Siobhan laughed.

I knew this was her way of blowing off the idea because she was scared that Tremaine wouldn't ask her out, after seeing how jealous she got when we saw him out Christmas shopping with the girl that turned out to be his cousin. It was up to me to bring the two of them together so that we could go out with a bang and enjoy that one night, worry-free. I was going to see to it that she had a great time for prom if it was the last thing I did.

CHAPTER 43

SIOBHAN

I couldn't let Carmen take her attention away from winning the fashion show, so I broke down and asked Mama for a few dollars. We went to our favorite Good Will store and sorted through all of the dresses that the rich folks so casually threw out. They all needed a little work, like beading, broken zippers, holes and splits way too high up the thigh.

"Let's do this. We find the cutest dresses we can, that don't have stains, and we take them home and make them our own. I'll do the sewing, but you have to get creative and figure out something different to do with your dress. Got it?" Carmen asked.

I nodded to assure her I would do my best to find the most beautiful gown for what was expected to be the best night of my life. I came across a red dress that hung to the floor. As I went to pick it up, another girl walked up and grabbed it at the same time. She was thinner and much shorter than me. It was going to take a lot of work to fit her in that gown, but it was already the perfect size for me.

It had the most beautiful neckline with a little room for cleavage and a high split over the left thigh. The shoulders fell just enough for my boobs to hold the entire dress up. Though the zipper and zipper track had been ripped off and there was a huge hole at the bottom, I knew there wasn't anything Mama or Carmen couldn't fix.

I let the girl go ahead and take the dress and I kept looking. Carmen shook her head at me. When I came across a very pretty black dress, she ripped it from my hands. "We're not going to a funeral, girl. Think red carpet. Think Hollywood. Think bigger!" Carmen said as she held a hot pink ruffled dress up to her chest. "How do I look?"

She made all kinds of faces like someone was taking pictures of her, and even did a fake laugh. It felt like the whole store was watching us as she put on a show. "Ooh!" she shouted as she ran over to a shoe rack by the wall. These would look great with this. What do you think?" she asked.

"I think…I think you look great in anything. You're lucky you're so small," I said

"Girl, you're fine just the way you are. You have a little extra to love, so it's going to take a little more time to pull your outfit together. Don't sweat it. I'm going to be one of the first designers to cater to full-figured girls and women. We're all beautiful, and when the fashion industry catches up, girl, this conversation will be a thing of the past. Watch."

I watched as she tried on a pair of sparkling silver pumps. I sat and looked at all of the beat-up dresses around me and started to feel hopeless. The girl who took my dress flopped around at the register, dancing, as the cashier rang them up and placed my dress neatly inside of a long, clear bag, by itself. She smiled even bigger as her mom pulled out her checkbook. Then, their faces changed. The dancing stopped, and the dress and bag were placed on the adjacent cash register.

They argued for a few seconds before the cashier started emptying one of their bags, putting the other items to the side with the dress. Then, her mom wrote another check, the cashier re-bagged their smaller items and they left. "I'll be back," I told Carmen. She was still in the mirror admiring herself as I power-walked to the front.

"Is this on hold?" I asked the cashier.

"We don't do holds. It's going back on the rack unless you want it," she said, smiling.

She passed me the dress and I held it up against my chest and began twirling in a circle. Carmen was finally ready to go, so we got in line. She gave my dress a weird look. "That's what you came up with?" she asked.

"It's not that bad. Really! You think you can make me look like Queen Latifah?" I asked, cheesing extra hard.

"I can do you one better," she replied. "I can make you look like Siobhan Butler. You'll be the hottest chick in the room. Boys will be lined up, waiting for a chance to dance with you."

"Dance?" I asked nervously.

"Yeah. What did you think happened at prom? People dance and have a good time. You thought you were about to go and just hold up the wall? Oh, no ma'am."

On the ride home, I psyched myself out thinking about guys asking me to dance. I couldn't do anything but the Tootsie Roll, the Butterfly, and the Macarena, and I only did that in my room. Heaven forbid they play anything slow. "I'm not going to prom," I said.

"What? What just happened? You were just so excited!"

"Carmen, I can't dance. I can't two-step. What if somebody does ask me to dance? Then what?"

"You get your butt on the dance floor and pretend to know what you're doing. You're thinking too much into this. Let's handle step one first. When we get your look down, I promise you won't be saying any of this."

I didn't say anything else for the rest of the ride. I drowned out my thoughts and the possibility of Carmen starting another conversation about prom, by blasting the music.

When we got home and tried on our dresses, I felt butterflies as I hid the flawed parts of the dress and held it up to my body while standing in the mirror. It fit every curve on my body, like I knew it would, and with the right girdle, my kangaroo pouch was going to be non-existent. I turned on the radio and practiced the Tootsie Roll with my dress on, to see how much room I had to move around and breathe. I felt like I had all of the rhythm in the world when I was in the comfort of my bedroom.

When Tremaine knocked, I freaked out and froze in place. "Come in," Carmen said, laughing and pushing me to the side. By the way he looked at me, I couldn't tell if he liked the dress or if he was trying to understand what was going on.

"Tremaine, your timing is impeccable. Siobhan and I were just talking about prom and we realized she doesn't have a date. Tell me, sir. Do you have a date for prom already?"

My heart was pounding, and I wanted to push Carmen's short tail off the bed. "Nah, I was actually thinking about asking you," he said, looking at me. Carmen just grinned like she had really done something special. "Who you going with?" he asked Carmen.

"I'll be going all by myself, thank you. Boys are too much trouble. Plus, I'm not trying to go to a hotel room with any of those little dusty boys at that school," she said.

"You never know. You might meet somebody at this party we got invited to," Tremaine said.

"A party? By who?" Carmen asked.

"My cousin, Whitney…this guy she's been seeing is throwing a house party for her birthday. So, y'all down? Siobhan?"

Everything in me wanted to say no, but I hadn't been to a party since I snuck out of the house during freshman year. "I'm down if you're down," Carmen said, giving me a goofy smile.

"I'm down," I said quickly before I had time to change my mind.

CHAPTER 44

TREMAINE

The last thing I expected when I asked the girls to go to this party with me was a no. I knew Siobhan was pretty shy and reserved and the party scene just wasn't her thing. I figured Carmen would've been down though. But honestly, I just wanted some time alone with Siobhan. Things had been weird with us since that kiss and making a move on her before graduation wasn't the smartest move. Unc was already on my back about choosing a school and keeping my nose clean, and that included any dealings with girls.

He knew he couldn't control my every move, so when I heard him asking Ms. Shanté over for dinner, I knew that was the perfect opportunity to ask about Whitney's birthday party. I hoped he would be so busy trying to pull off a fly fit to show off his lack of style, hoping to hide his lack of game, that he didn't realize what I'd just asked him, until I was dressed and ready to go. Before I closed the door behind me, he said, "Be home by 11:00.

I walked past Ms. Shanté on my way to Siobhan's car. "Where's little man?" I asked.

"He's fine. You go have fun. Take care of my baby, please," she replied.

Carmen was hanging out of the window, beating on the side of the car, yelling, "Let's go! It's time to party!" They put me in the backseat again, so that Selena Jr. could control the radio and make our ears bleed while sounding like a wounded wolf.

"Who sings this?" I asked.

"Man, this my girl, Christina! I'm a genie in a bottle, baby!" she sang.

"Oh, I just thought you would let her sing it, since it seems she knows ALL the lyrics."

Siobhan tried to hide the fact that she was laughing by looking out of the window. It only made Carmen sing even louder to every song that came on the radio after that. "Yo, make this next right," I shouted.

Siobhan finally turned the radio down as we pulled up to the party. She shut the engine off and we all sat there and watched the folks going in, and the guys hanging around the door. "Alright, we need a code word for when it's time to go," I suggested. The girls looked at each other, then at me like I was crazy.

"A code word? Is it something you need to tell us before we go up in here with all these folks we don't know?" Carmen asked.

"I trust you," Siobhan said, smiling.

"That's all fine and dandy, but why do we need a code word?" Carmen interrupted.

"Look, I don't know all these folks. My cousin invited us, and I thought it'd be cool for us to get out of the house. If they start to get rowdy, we out. We good?

"Yeah," Carmen said.

Once we got past the fake ass bouncers holding down the front door, the party seemed kind of chill. A few girls were grinding on their dudes. The air was thick from the cigarette smoke and weed in the air, and 40 oz. bottles were all over the tables and floor around the couch. Siobhan and Carmen grabbed onto me as we walked around looking for Whitney. Siobhan grabbed my arm tighter as we got to the backyard. The music was blasting and the light from the pool was the only way I was able to see Whitney across the yard, sitting on some dude's lap.

"You good? I asked Siobhan.

She loosened her grip just a little but never let go. She looked like she'd seen a ghost when Whitney basically leaped over the swimming pool and hugged me like we were best friends. She knocked me right into a guy with a joint in his hand. "Damn, man! Watch what you doin'!" he said, stepping up in my face.

"Hey! Back up, Knuckle. This is my baby cuz I was telling you about," Whitney said.

I could tell homeboy was used to people backing down when he bucked up, but I ain't never been scared of nobody, and I wasn't making an exception for him. I didn't flinch when he pressed his chest up against mine. I felt the girls pull on my arm, so I stepped back.

"Can we go now?" Siobhan asked.

"Girl, we just got here," Carmen said.

"Let me talk to my cuz for a minute. I'm not feeling this either," I replied.

I wasn't driving and if Siobhan didn't feel safe, I wasn't about to stick around just to prove I could protect her. But right as we were about to head out, Whitney's boyfriend walked up.

"Tremaine…Tremaine's friends, this is my boyfriend, Buck," Whitney said, as she hung onto his neck, kissing the tattoos all over the side of his face. I felt weird watching Buck stare at Siobhan.

"Don't I know you?" he asked her.

"Tremaine, can we please go now?" she insisted.

"Yeah, I'm ready," Carmen agreed.

I reached out to give Whitney a hug before we left, and she put on the most pitiful face and gave me a little pat on the back.

"What's the hurry? Buck asked.

I didn't feel like explaining myself to him or anybody there, but I could feel some kind of awkward tension building, so I played it cool.

"My girl ain't feeling good. We just stopped by to say hey to my cousin. That's it. Y'all have a good night," I said.

Whitney looked like she was enjoying every bit of her boyfriend sizing me up and me trying to get out of there. I left trouble in Louisiana, and Unc told me if I got arrested out here, I was on my own.

"You say this your girl, huh? This pretty chocolate thang right here?" he asked, stepping up to move Siobhan's braids off her shoulder.

"Alright, cuz. I'll catch up with you later," Whitney said, looking up beside Buck's head.

"Siobhan, right?" Buck asked.

I tried to act like it wasn't bothering me that he was stopping us from leaving. But he crossed the line by getting in Siobhan's face. "Like I said, we about to be out. My girl ain't feeling good. Good night," I said, stepping in front of Siobhan.

"That's funny. The last time I saw her, she was my girl. I almost caught a charge off her lyin' ass," he said.

"Watch ya mouth," I said, pushing Carmen and Siobhan back. He yelled over my shoulder toward her.

"Oh, you ain't tell lil' man, huh? Yeah, she lied about being 18 after she snuck into the club and then took me back to her crib and let me handle that. You know what's funny though? A few months later, she claimed she was pregnant, when I wouldn't talk to her no more," Buck continued.

I started backing up and we headed for the exit. The closer we got to the front door, the faster we started moving. He was right on our tails and Whitney was on his, screaming and acting a fool. He passed me trying to catch up with Siobhan and had the guys at the door grab me. He grabbed her arm and yanked her around. Carmen jumped on his back as I wrestled my way out of the other guy's grip.

I kept a pocketknife on me since Unc made me toss my gun in the Red River before we left Louisiana. When I managed to tear away from them, I punched the big one in the throat and pinned the thin one against the wall. "We ain't come here for no problems," I said. After I felt like they got my message, I let him go and ran over to the girls.

Carmen managed to get Buck down on the ground beside a broken-down car in the yard. I could see his eyes rolling into the back of his head, and somehow, I managed to pull her from around his neck and we hopped in the car, then burned out. Siobhan kept checking the rearview mirror, hoping they didn't follow us.

She drove around for a little while before finally pulling over at a nearby beach. The moon lit our path to a spot near a group of people wrapping up a bonfire. The sounds of the waves crashing against each other drowned out the awkward silence between us. Siobhan ran ahead of us, toward the water. She was walking beyond the shoreline when we caught up to her.

She pulled away from me when I tried to touch her. Carmen stepped up and grabbed her arm, pulling her back, and they just stood there and hugged. I wanted them to know

I had their backs, so I sat between them, in the sand, trying to keep them warm.

We spent the rest of the night just standing in the ocean, holding hands. When the breeze became too much for us, and none of us had a jacket, we headed back to the car. Siobhan stopped behind us.

"I need to tell y'all something," she said.

Me and Carmen went back and sat in the sand. Carmen leaned on my shoulder as Siobhan said her peace.

"I haven't been honest with either of you. I've been carrying on with a lie because I was scared of what y'all might think if you knew the truth about me. Buck wasn't lying. I did meet him when I was in ninth grade. Some old friends helped me get a fake ID so we could sneak in the club. One lie led to another and I lost my virginity to a man who hates me. Luckily, my mama came home. When she threatened to call the police, he left.

When I told him I was pregnant, he threatened to have me killed if I didn't get an abortion, because he said he wasn't going to jail behind me. While I was away at a home for pregnant teens, Mama picked up and moved us far away from him. When I had Chase, we decided to pass him off as my little brother," she said.

Little did she know, I kind of already assumed Chase was her kid, or that Ms. Shanté was just one of those parents who put their kids on autopilot. Carmen looked like she was unsure about how to receive everything Siobhan said.

"That had to be hard, keeping that secret and being scared to live your life for all these years like that," I said.

She finally stopped crying, and said, "I just hate that you guys had to find out this way. I should've said something sooner. Carmen, remind me to call you the next time somebody's trying to fight," she said, laughing and wiping her tears.

"You better call me, shoot," Carmen said.

"I'll be right there too," I said.

"And girl, there was no way for you to know his cousin was hooking up with your ex. Plus, we haven't been friends that long. You didn't owe us that explanation. You think I would've told anybody I had a kid in high school, much less that somebody wanted me dead because of it?" Carmen asked.

Carmen grabbed Siobhan's hand and we headed back toward the car. "From now on, we tell each other the truth, even if it hurts," Carmen said.

"I agree," I said.

"Me too," Siobhan added.

CHAPTER 45

CARMEN

When the students participating in the fashion show were released from class for practice, some of the male teachers and students put the stage together while the rest of the crew checked the curtains and lights. The rest of us did a dress rehearsal in the back as chaos ensued.

Siobhan was super late to practice, so we barely had time to work on her walk for the show. Tremaine was there, front and center, parading back and forth across the stage. All of the models for the other designers were standing around smiling and practically drooling. I couldn't tell if it was because he had a dip to his walk or if they thought he was cute.

Siobhan only had time to change into the one-piece swimsuit. She didn't make it out onto the stage before her ankles buckled and she hit the floor. She cried so loud, everybody stopped laughing and started helping her up.

When she got home from the doctor, my worst fears were confirmed. She had sprained her ankle and backed out of the show. Part of me wanted to believe she was relieved because she wasn't at all excited about being my main model anymore.

"I'm really sorry. You know I wanted to be there for you, she said," propping her leg up on a pillow.

"It's okay. I just hope I have time to find somebody else."

I tried to keep my composure, but I was breaking inside. I had worked hard on those pieces for her and with the show just weeks away, it was back out or break down and ask somebody else to take her place. "Where's Chase's sleeping clothes?" I asked.

Bathing Chase was a nice break from everything else going on. He put a pile of bubbles on his face and mocked Santa Claus. "Ho, Ho, Ho," he said, laughing. He had the cutest little smile. Later he fell asleep in my arms, and every time I moved, he would wake up.

When Ms. Shanté came home from work and checked in on us, she took over. "Tiring, ain't it?" she asked. I wiped the half-dried slob from my chin as she sat down beside me. "Siobhan told me she told you and Tremaine about Chase. I never thought that I would be a grandmother this young. As embarrassing as it is for her, it is equally as embarrassing for me. When I tried to explain that to her, she couldn't understand where I was coming from. Hopefully, you can, since you both are so close now. She's never had a real friend before. You coming to stay here was truly a blessing for all of us," she said.

I didn't like to get mixed up in their business, but I could see why she would've been embarrassed about the whole situation. "Mami told me when she met you, she felt the same way about being pregnant with me. She said the last thing she ever wanted was to bring a kid in this world without a husband to help her, and that you had her back from the time you guys met. I just wanted to return the favor. Siobhan needs all the love she can get, since she doesn't know how to give it to herself," I told her.

"You're pretty mature for your age," she replied.

"I never had any other choice. When Mami started changing, I had to grow up fast so I could take care of myself. I don't know what happened to her."

"Look, maybe you'll understand one day when you have kids. Sometimes being a single parent just gets a little too hard for some parents to bear. Now, there's no excuse for her just completely walking away. But something had to happen for her to just up and change on you. Have you ever asked her?"

"We never talk about anything anymore. She wants to talk about her boyfriends. I want to talk about college. We're on two different levels. She doesn't understand me," I said, starting to get angry.

"What about college? You know where you want to go?"

"Well, I'm hoping to win this scholarship so I can go to NYU."

"You're going all the way to New York to be by yourself? Have you ever looked into the Fashion Institute of Design and Merchandising right here at home?" she asked.

I had looked into it, but I wanted to get far away from LA. I had gone through enough in California and I wanted something new. When she finally got up to go to bed, I fell asleep considering staying in Cali for college. I knew it wouldn't be so bad after I was finally in my own place. But I had just spent the last five years of my life preparing for New York and deciding not to go felt like I was giving up on myself, and I just couldn't do that.

CHAPTER 46

SIOBHAN

As I sat on my bed, looking at college applications, feeling the weight of the world on my shoulders, I couldn't help but think about if a career in acting might work out. For the sake of Chase, I applied for at least two local colleges with no plans to immediately declare a concentration, but I at least wanted to give it a shot, just in case my dreams didn't work out. I couldn't see myself cleaning up behind people for the rest of my life like Mama. I wanted more. I wanted excitement. I wanted everything people thought I didn't deserve because of one bad decision.

Having a baby at 14 and keeping him a secret didn't mean I was free of judgment and people's dirty looks. I could tell some people knew he was mine when we were out in public. The white women were the worst. They would pull their daughters closer and lecture them right in my face. Mama told me the day I had him that no excuse would ever be good enough for the world when it came to teen pregnancy. If I was a victim of rape, the media would've said it was because of how I was dressed. If I was molested, Mama would be blamed for not being home enough. Or they would just assume my dad wasn't in my life.

The funny thing was though, the person that I assumed would instantly pull away from me asked me on a real date for my 18th birthday just days after finding out the truth about me. Carmen didn't see it as a big deal and even started helping me out more around the house. I even started to notice a change in how she treated me about having to take him with us when we went places together. At the movies, we would take turns taking him out in the hall if he cried. She would help me feed him and get him ready for bed, and she even agreed to babysit for my birthday date.

She helped me pick out a nice but simple denim dress and painted my nails while she gave me tips on what not to do. "How many dates have you been on?" I asked. She shook her head and just laughed.

"I've never been on a real date. My only real boyfriend just wanted to sit in the park in the dark and kiss. Every time he would reach for my thigh, I would pop his knuckles with a small wave brush I always kept in my purse. I would laugh hysterically when I got home because he never knew what it was, and he thought I was playing with him every time I told him to stop touching certain parts of my body. After a while, it stopped being funny though. No other guys ever wanted to date me. They only saw a big butt and long hair and wanted one thing," she continued. "So, I cut my hair and started wearing baggy clothes, hoping that one day I would just disappear."

When she finished my nails and I had my outfit on, Chase ran up to me and hugged my legs as I admired my lips and shimmering skin in the mirror. Then, Mama came around the corner and just stood there and watched me pin my braids up. "You look beautiful," she said. I gave her the biggest hug and the wettest kiss right above the beauty mark near her top lip.

"Thank you," I said as Carmen had to pull herself away from her Peeping Tom position, over Mama's shoulder, to go answer the door for Tremaine.

I started getting nervous, so Mama gave me a napkin to wipe off my lip gloss. You're turning 18 tomorrow. I think it's time for a little more color. She went into her room and came back with a green tube. It was the lipstick I used to play in as a kid, from Avon, that was green in the tube but turned a bold red after a few minutes. Suddenly, my teeth shined a little brighter and my nerves turned into confidence as I limped on my crutches to my date, who was standing just a few feet away, with his mouth wide open.

He looked so nice with his fresh haircut, and he even bought a new gold chain to match a new pair of gold earrings. "You are gorgeous," he said, smiling from ear to ear. Then, Uncle Tony appeared from the kitchen, eating a piece of cold leftover fried chicken.

"Hey, now. Don't do anything I wouldn't do tonight. And be back by 11," Uncle Tony said.

I tossed my keys to Tremaine and we left for a night out on the town. He drove me to the Santa Monica Pier where we rode the Pacific Park Ferris Wheel twice, while my heart melted as I laid in his arms. He smelled like cocoa butter with a hint of Polo. When we talked, the vibration of his deep voice and his beard tickled the side of my face, so I moved my head down to his chest.

He went on and on about something I can't even remember because the sound of his heartbeat consumed me. That, along with the cool breeze coming off of the water nearly put me to sleep. When the ride stopped, I watched him try to win me a huge *Winnie the Pooh* stuffed bear. After losing about $20, he was successful, and he even carried it to the car for me, where we sat in the parking lot, on the hood of my car, and shared a funnel cake. "You got something on your face," he said, as he leaned in and gently dusted powdered sugar from my chin.

"May I?" he asked. I leaned in and met him halfway as our lips locked and fireworks crackled in the night sky. His lips were just as soft as they were the first time and this kiss lasted longer and was much more romantic. I didn't want the night to end.

When we got back to the house, we sat in the driveway for a few minutes. Neither of us spoke as we smiled and avoided eye contact. He reached over and pulled my hand up to his lips, kissing me along my arm.

"So...," he started.

I gave him my undivided attention, as my face began to hurt from smiling so much. "Will you be my girl now?"

Instead of responding, I started trying to climb out. He hopped out and ran around to my side to help me. Before we went back inside, I kissed him again and whispered in his ear, "I thought you'd never ask".

Then, the door swung open, and Carmen stood there, with Chase on her hip. "So, how was it?" she asked.

"It felt like I was in a dream," I gushed, as we went inside, and he and his uncle left. I relived that night in my head every night before bed for at least the next month.

CHAPTER 47

TREMAINE

I couldn't stop thinking about that night Siobhan became my lady. When this older lady came in the shop to pawn her engagement ring, my brain switched gears. "Don't worry. I won't be coming back for it," she said, slamming it on the counter. I could feel Unc breathing down my neck, as I checked the ring out. The lady just stood there, fuming, as I passed it over my shoulder.

"Will $100 do?" Unc asked.

"I would've taken $10 for the piece of shit. So, yes. I will gladly take $100," she replied.

Uncle Tony passed her a form to fill out and patted me on the shoulder as he walked away. When she left, I couldn't help but to stare at it in the glass case underneath the cash register, then I took it out to get a closer look. Unc spooked me when he took it out of my hand and put it back in the case, slamming and locking the door.

"Don't be getting any ideas. You need to slow down," he said, as he walked over to the front door, watching people passed by.

"What idea is that?" I asked, coming from behind the counter.

"Look, the girl has a kid. You want to be baby daddy number two?"

"Unc, I know you mean well, but I'm not about to let you talk about her like that. That's my lady now. I don't disrespect whatever this whole thing is between you and her mom, and as a man, I deserve the same respect for my relationship."

"A man? You think you're a man now? You don't know the first thing about being a man. A man handles his business," he boasted.

At that point I was getting pissed, because I felt like he was testing me.

"That's actually why I'm planning to buy that ring we just took in. I'm a man of my word, and soon enough she'll know. So will you."

He walked up in my face like he wanted to fight me. Then, he laughed and brushed past me. "Something funny?" I asked. He threw his hand up and went to the back and closed the door.

Right before he pulled the drawer for the night, I walked around to the other side, pulled out my wallet and slammed it on the glass. "The ring, please?" He shook his head, scoffing, as his nostrils grew.

"You really about to blow $200 on a ring for a girl you barely know, who hid a whole kid from you?" he asked.

"The ring, please!" I insisted.

"Tremaine, you graduate in what, three months? How many times have I asked you about applying to college? Have you even thought about how y'all will handle a relationship when you leave?"

"You say that like she can't go to college because she has a son. Women do it all the time," I said.

He took my money and pushed the ring across the counter, then pulled the drawer. I locked up the store and sat outside on the sidewalk, waiting for him to come out. When he didn't come out about ten minutes after shutting off all the lights, I went back in. He was sitting at his desk, holding a

251

wallet-sized picture. "Unc, can we go now? I got a test tomorrow," I said.

He just focused on the picture, and I think I even saw a tear form in his eyes. He went to stuff it in his pocket and headed toward the door. The picture fell on the floor and I waited until he was a few steps ahead of me before picking it up and sticking it in my back pocket.

CHAPTER 48

CARMEN

"Coming to the stage, the beautiful, vibrant designs of the one and only, Bella Valentina! And the crowd goes wild!" Ms. Shanté shouted, as she and Chase cheered and stuffed their faces with popcorn, while Siobhan strolled down the hall on her one good leg, through the living room.

The seamstress in me was watching her every move. The last thing I wanted was to have her get on stage and have a malfunction halfway through her walk. Everything seemed to be fitting pretty well and she seemed to be more confident in the outfits, especially the swimwear pieces. When she got to the end of the plastic runner leading to the front door, she turned and twisted her ankle again.

"Ouch!" she shouted.

Ms. Shanté and I ran over to help her to the couch. "Girl, are you sure you can do this? I don't know if you will be ready in a couple of weeks," I said. Her mom could see the concern on my face.

"I have an idea," she said. "Why don't you have Tremaine carry her down the aisle for the swimwear section of the show? She can walk on her own for the other styles, but you could make it a little cute with them walking down together. I mean, they do have matching swimwear, right?"

My face lit up! That would be perfect! That way Siobhan wouldn't be on her feet as much and it would add a little something to our segment. The excitement overwhelmed me, and I almost forgot that I had to run out to the fabric store to get more material for Siobhan's sarong.

"Go straight there and back," Ms. Shanté said. "You know you don't have a license yet and the police have been hot this week.

I got in and out of the store faster than I expected and decided to grab a bite to eat. I could tell a storm was moving in, so I called in my order to my favorite Mexican spot. When I walked outside, André was standing outside leaning against the back of Siobhan's car. "What's up? I see you out here doing good. You lookin' good. Can I get a ride?" he asked.

"No, but you can move your ass so I can go. And why are you out here waiting on me anyway? I made it clear the last time I saw you that I want nothing to do with you," I hissed.

My attitude always turned him on, unless he was getting clowned in front of his boys or the whole school. He wanted to be cool so bad. "I miss you. Why you leave Beachwood?" he asked.

"Why are you so worried about me? I'm not checking up on you, so let me be, okay?"

"Ma, you know I got mad love for you. Let me take you out some time," he said, grinning like that was supposed to impress me.

"André, take your ass on up the street to wherever you were going before I call the police."

Then, he jumped back up on the sidewalk. "Yo, chill. You don't need to do all that. Why you hate me so much?"

"Oh, so you don't remember? Because I remember very clearly what you did to me last summer. You never even apologized," I said, beginning to choke up.

"Apologize for what? You came on to me. I just gave you what you wanted. You can't just stop me from doing my thing when it's just getting good. Why you even come over?"

I ignored his response and got in the car and started it up. He stood in front of it and slammed his hands on the hood. "Get out the car and talk to me. I ain't finished with you yet," he shouted. I kept the car in park and mashed the gas. I saw a small amount of fear in his eyes, so I finally put it in drive. When he didn't budge, I pressed the gas lightly. He hit the hood again. Without thinking, I mashed it harder, and his ass jumped up on the sidewalk and I sped off.

As soon as I pulled off, he kicked the bumper of the car. I was tired of being pushed around, so I slammed on the brakes. He walked around to the driver's side window and I got out, stomped him right in the balls, and emptied my drink out on him.

"Remember this day the next time you decide to fuck with me," I said sternly. I politely got back in the car and drove off with Ms. Shanté 's *Waiting to Exhale* soundtrack on repeat.

As I came through the door, I tossed Siobhan her keys and a few dollars for the damage, went to the room and buried my face in a pillow. I screamed and cried until I was almost certain my rage had subsided. Siobhan came hopping in the room and laid down beside me. "Want to talk about it?" she asked. I turned over on my back and slid over closer to her as she wrapped her arm around my neck.

"What would you do if somebody hurt you and you were afraid to tell anybody?" I asked.

"How would this person have hurt me?"

"When you had your first time, did it hurt?"

"Yeah," she responded, this time turning over to face me. "Did yours?"

"Yeah. I asked him to stop, but he kept going. When I tried to get up, he held my arms down until he was done. Then, he kissed me and got dressed to leave. I felt so dirty and embarrassed, and I was hurting. Mami came home late that night and I just didn't know what to do. I didn't know what to say. I mean, I wasn't even supposed to be at his house. People always say I'm mean and angry for no reason. I just can't keep letting people get away with hurting me. You ever felt like that?" I asked.

"Well, my first time wasn't very memorable. I didn't even want to do it, but I was scared to say no. I felt like it was my fault for lying about my age, so I just thought I deserved anything that happened to me that night. I lied to my mama and said I was going to a sleepover. I didn't know how to talk to her about it. I knew she would be mad and probably even kick me out. She always threatened to send me to live with my daddy. So, I just kept it to myself. When my period didn't show up, I started to freak out," she said.

"I'm sorry that happened to you," I told her.

"I'm sorry he hurt you. You didn't deserve that," she said.

"You know, I ran into him today? He wouldn't leave me alone, so I did what I had to do. Sorry about your car," I said, laughing.

"It's okay. It's raggedy anyway. Besides, he deserved it. Next time, tell somebody," Siobhan said.

"Somebody like who?" I asked.

"Start with me, and we'll figure it out from there."

CHAPTER 49

SIOBHAN

After putting Chase down for the night, I stood in the mirror and carefully examined every part of my body, especially the stretchmarks on my sides, from my pregnancy. I panicked at the thought of the whole school seeing my life's story all over my body while I attempted step outside of my comfort zone.

The next day, Tremaine invited me over for a study session while Uncle Tony was at work. It was clear he knew what he was doing and just needed an excuse to get me there, but I couldn't be mad at that. While I was lying across the bed, my shirt came untucked from my jean jumper and a fat roll exposed itself. I jumped up and stuffed everything back in as soon as I noticed it.

"You sure you're gonna be able to pull off this fashion show?" he asked. You know you have a choice, right?"

"Yeah. I just don't want to disappoint Carmen. I know she wants and needs this scholarship. I can't let her down like that," I replied.

He pulled my shirt back out of my overalls and gently ran his hand across my waist. "Your body is banging," he said, smiling, as he moved his hands closer to the sides of my jumpsuit that were lined with buttons.

All of the worries of my heart ceased to exist when he wrapped his arms around me and kissed me. Our tongues danced the night away as his grip on my waist tightened and the straps of my jumper came undone. When he climbed on top of me, he leaned down and lined my neck with kisses. Then, I started having flashbacks of Buck, and my body stiffened.

"What's wrong?" he asked softly, watching my lips as I responded.

"It's nothing," I lied.

"You sure? We can stop, if you want."

I couldn't continue to lie to him, so I laid there, twirling a braid around my fingers. Then, when we heard a knock at the door pulled us out of that very moment when we started fixing our clothes, as Uncle Tony walked in. Tremaine was still in bed beside me, causing his uncle to grow angrier by the second.

"You need to go," he told me. I did as I was told and grabbed my shoes and ran. From the parking lot, I could hear them arguing.

After I left, I rode around the neighborhood a few times so I could calm down before going home. I knew it was only a matter of time before Mr. Tony got on the phone to snitch to Mama. When I walked in the door, Carmen instantly caught on to the fact that something was going on. She turned the tv off and followed me to the room. "Girl, spill," she said, gushing. I was in no mood to have one of our girly, boy-crazed chats, but out of nowhere, it came out.

"Tremaine's uncle walked in on us."

CHAPTER 50

TREMAINE

For the last two days, Unc avoided me at all costs. When I would wake up for school, he would already be gone to work, he was always getting off as I was coming in and if he did speak, it would be brief and work-related. When I slid a flyer under his bedroom door for the fashion show, he opened before I stood up. I passed it to him and asked, "think you'll make it?" He laughed in my face and brushed past me, bumping my shoulder.

"Yo, what is your problem with me?" I yelled, approaching him from behind.

When he turned around, I was right in his face, staring down at him, attitude on 1,000. "You think you grown? You think you about to lay up with some girl in my house, where I pay the bills? Then, you have the nerve to buck up to me and question me about the lil' hoodrat?" He shouted.

I backed up when I felt spit hit the side of my face. "I'm only asking you one more time. Watch ya mouth when you talkin' about my lady."

"Your lady huh? Well, answer me this… Why does "your lady" have more miles on her than my ride outside? You're doing all this over a girl that laid down with some good for nothing ass thug and made a baby, that she kept a secret from you. Now you're defending her honor?"

With my chest pressed against his, I pulled the picture he dropped at the shop from my pocket. "Why you so bent out of shape about what I do and who I do it with? Siobhan is nothing but nice to you. She's a great girl. And so what she had a damn baby? You're still holding onto the fact ya old lady left you for some dude and stuck you with the child support. Yeah, didn't think I knew, did you? You played yourself. So, don't blame me because it ain't work out for you. Siobhan is different. But you wouldn't know nothing about that," I said, throwing the picture in his face.

He picked it up, looked at it for a minute, then threw it back at me. "You lost your damn mind?" he asked, then, he laid my ass out. We tore that apartment up. He took a cheap shot and got me right in my mouth, busting my damn lip. He came at me while I was getting up, and when I moved out of the way, he crashed into the wall. When the iron flew past my face, I knew he had lost his mind. I grabbed my shit and I left.

When I walked up the sidewalk to Siobhan's house, something came over me and I stopped dead in my tracks. I sat on the sidewalk for a minute and cried to myself. I couldn't let anyone else see me weak, especially my baby. After I finally calmed down, I saw her leaving with Chase. Before she got in, she looked up and our eyes met. I just stood there as more tears fell down my face. My lip burned and my face was throbbing. And all I wanted at that moment was for somebody to listen to hold me. She took Chase back out and headed my way. I hurried and cleaned my face before they made it over to me.

"What's going on? Why are you sitting out here?" she asked. "And what happened to your face?"

She pulled a wet wipe from her bag and started cleaning my cuts. That made everything sting. When she held my face and softly blew into a cut on the side of my eye, she stared into my soul, then wrapped her arms around me. I held her so tight that I didn't want to let go.

Siobhan represented so many things in my life, but one thing she gave me that nobody else did was hope. When I was with her, I felt like I could take on the world.

When we were apart, I counted the days and the moments when I would see her again. I hated that her mom and Uncle Tony tried to keep us apart while they played house behind our backs.

"Where y'all headed?" I asked, pulling her away from me so I could get another look at her.

"I just wanted to get out of the house. Mama been tripping lately. Carmen is focused on the fashion show. Just needed some air. Wanna ride with us?"

Instead of waiting for a response, she took my hand and led me to her car. I filled up her tank and we rode around until Chase fell asleep, then pulled over at a park. I pushed her on the swings and watched her smile. They slept on the drive home. When we got a few blocks from the house, Siobhan woke up and held my hand as the slow jams countdown on the radio was slowly coming to an end. "I'm sorry," she said.

"Sorry for what? You didn't do anything wrong."

"I knew better. We knew better. I just got caught up in the moment. I don't want you or Uncle Tony thinking I'm trying to trap you."

"Why would you say something like that?" I asked. I was getting angry, but it wasn't at her. Everything in me wanted another go with Unc.

"I love you. I would never want to cost you your dreams or the plans you have for your future. I know dating a girl with a baby isn't easy."

"It's nothing I've never seen before. Don't trip. My uncle just bitter because he got played when he was our age and he never got over it. That don't got nothing to do with us."

I pulled into the driveway and kissed her before she disappeared inside. On my walk back home, I said a prayer and hoped Unc had calmed down so I could get some sleep. The iron was still in the same spot. There was a hole where he ran into the wall. Blood had dried up in small puddles in the carpet and a picture frame that held the last picture of my ma, granny and Uncle Tony was shattered. My room was still intact, but there was a perfectly placed letter on my bed that read, "You need to find your own place after graduation." I knew things were bad, but I wasn't ready to live on my own. But he left me no choice.

CHAPTER 51

CARMEN

The day had finally arrived, everybody was scrambling backstage. Models and clothes were everywhere. The air smelled like Spritz and Oil Sheen, and the sounds of heels clacking against the wooden floor gave me a rush. Ms. Shanté was working overtime on Siobhan's makeup and pinning her hair up. Tremaine was helping to add some bling to her cast. The DJ was getting the audience hype as they came in. I tried to get a peek at the judge's table, but it was empty. Three trophies sat near the edge, with three white envelopes leaning against each of them.

"Alright, how much longer on hair and makeup?" I asked. Siobhan's face was sour from her mom pulling too hard on her braids.

"Five more minutes," Ms. Shanté said.

"Tremaine, what are we looking like on the cast?"

He looked at me and held up his hands, that were covered in glitter, glue and rhinestones. I wanted to laugh, but the drama teacher, Mrs. McMillan, charged through the changing areas shouting, "Ten minutes people! The show starts in 10 minutes. Have your models ready and lined up if you're in the first segment."

My stomach felt like someone had stuck a knife and a handful of pins through it. "I got this," I whispered to myself.

"You really think so? Brandy asked, with a devilish grin on her face. "See, my dad paid a real seamstress to put my pieces together. I'm sure the Salvation Army will accept yours though. Those poor people. What was I thinking? Even a homeless person wouldn't wear this mess. But carry on."

"Break a leg," I said, followed by a serious prayer that she would.

The DJ cut the music and I could hear Mrs. McMillan shouting to the crowd. "Are you ready? Our students have worked really hard to put on a great show for you guys, all for the chance at a full ride to the college of their choosing. Please join me in welcoming our judges. We're pleased that you've joined us at Pulliam Preparatory Academy's 3rd Annual Spring Fashion Show! Without further ado, please stand to your feet and welcome to the stage, our first collection, BBG by Brandy Bonds. The crowd went bananas as her models flaunted an array of different neon-colored sundresses. Some were so short that they stopped just below the girl's butts and the others were so long that they had to hold the trains to keep from falling."

The music was feeding the crowd's excitement as Brandy's models came off and DeAnna's group went next. I looked over at Siobhan who looked petrified and about ready to throw up. "It's now or never," I told her. When it was time for us to line up, the crowd's cheering died down a little as Siobhan hopped out there on her blinged-out crutches, rocking a pair of denim bell bottoms with a red hot bustier, giving all kinds of attitude on the runway. Ms. Shanté peeked through the curtains and watched her, with a huge smile on her face.

Tremaine burst through the curtains behind Siobhan and gave her the sexiest look as he strolled past her, licking his lips, then dipped extra hard, before ripping his shirt open at the end of the runway. His khaki linen pants clung to his waist as he spun around on his heels to show off the Bella Valentina logo on the back of his shirt. The girls went crazy and rushed the staged as he egged them on. "Ladies and gentlemen, that wraps up our spring collections. Up next, summer. And my, my, my is it getting hot in here!" Mrs. McMillan said.

Tremaine ran backstage to change, and the crowd was still going crazy as the show went on. Siobhan was getting frustrated and struggling to get into her one piece. Tremaine held her up while her mom helped her get inside. We laughed as Ms. Shanté made Tremaine close his eyes and turn his back. "Okay, we're done," Siobhan said, rolling her eyes at her mom. Tremaine took off his linen pants to reveal a pair of lime green and orange trunks with a yellow BV stitched at the bottom of the left leg, in cursive. I lathered him down in baby oil, as Siobhan watched cautiously.

"Girl, I don't want Tremaine's crusty behind," I said, jokingly. "No offense, Tremaine."

"None taken, he said, kissing Siobhan in the top of her head.

When it was time for them to line up again, Siobhan went out without the crutches, rocking one yellow pump with her blinged-out cast. Halfway down the runway, Tremaine walked up behind her sporting his swimming trunks, a wife-beater that was ripped at the chest, and a pair of black thong sandals. Siobhan posed seductively at the end of the runway and waited. Tremaine posed right next to her as cameras flashed and girls screamed and cheered. Then, Tremaine swooped her up into his arms, posed for the flashing cameras, then glided off the stage.

Brandy was fuming and I couldn't help but laugh in her face. At that moment, the satisfaction that I got from watching her jaw hit the floor made my day. For as long as I'd known Brandy, she always thought she deserved more than everybody. Somehow, I felt sorry for her because she had never really felt comfortable being herself, and when we were friends, I could sense that she had some issues she didn't want to deal with. I tried to be there for her, but she chose a different route, and I couldn't do anything about that.

The show took a brief intermission and when it was just me and Siobhan in our section, I let out a huge sigh of relief and fell on her shoulder. Every part of my body hurt, and I was ready for it all to be over.

"So, did he tell your mom?" I asked her.

"I don't know. She hasn't said anything. At this point, I don't care if she knows. I'm 18 now. I can handle myself," she replied.

Tremaine returned with a few bottles of water and sat on the floor beside us. "So, how are we doing?" he asked.

"Not too bad. Brandy's pretty pissed. But…I can't tell if the crowd loves my pieces or the show you two have been putting on."

"Sorry," Siobhan said, trying to get to the itch inside of her cast.

Tremaine pulled a ruler from their bag and handed it to her. Her eyes rolled into the back of her head as the ruler disappeared inside of her cast and she scratched for what seemed like an hour. We laughed together until Brandy walked up. She stuck out her hand while smacking on a piece of gum, looking at everybody but me. "That supposed to mean something to me?" I asked.

"Just…you did a good job. If I lose, I'm fine losing to you. Just, don't tell anyone I was nice to you. Okay? I got a reputation to keep."

"That's you being nice? Girl, whatever you're selling, I'm not buying. Good luck," I said, laughing.

She stormed off to her section as the show started back up. "This is our last look. We pull this off and Siobhan, I do your chores for a week."

"Make it a month," she said, as she leaned on Tremaine trying to stand up.

"Okay, a month."

"What about me?" Tremaine asked.

"I can…I can help you get fly for prom…I know you're tight on cash. I know this. I got you!" I insisted.

"Yeah, we'll see," he laughed.

"Let's make this one count," I said, fixing Tremaine's

white and black blazer and black slacks.

Siobhan readjusted herself in a light-weight black, pleated skirt, with a sleeveless white blouse and sparkling black headband. Everybody lined up for the final walk-through and I felt a lump rise in my throat. "Breathe," Siobhan said, as she grabbed my hand. The line started moving and when the warmth of the spotlight hit my face, I showed the audience every tooth in my mouth. The three of us posed together while everybody nearly blinded us with their flashes.

"Would all designers please step forward?" Mrs. McMillan asked.

Tremaine and Siobhan fell back with the rest of the models, lined up across the stage. Kimora entered stage right, and Alicia entered stage left. I tried to remain calm, but my sweaty hands were a dead giveaway. I quickly wiped them on my trousers just in time to shake each of the ladies' hands.

"Let's hear it for these amazing designers!" Kimora said.

The crowd cheered and calmed back down as the ladies were handed the trophies and envelopes. I looked back at Siobhan and Tremaine who were holding hands. Together, they waved at me, then Tremaine winked and Siobhan blew me a kiss.

"And now, the moment you've all been waiting for!

In third place, we have, Sheena Nngawa!" Alicia said.

My stomach and butt cheeks tightened in the moments before Sheena's name was called. She smiled as she accepted her certificate and trophy, but I could see the tears trying to escape her eyes.

"In second place, congratulations to…Carmen Martinez!"

My heart sunk and all I could hear was Mami's voice saying repeatedly, "Good things don't happen for people like you and me". I managed to keep my composure until Kimora announced Brandy as the winner. I began to feel faint, so I skipped the photos and ran to the car where I sat on the hood and replayed the entire show in my head.

Siobhan came out a few minutes behind me, still dressed in the last style. "How are you holding up?" she asked. I wiped the wet mascara from my cheeks and slid down off the car.

"I just want to go home."

"Tremaine's grabbing the rest of our things and we can go. Carmen, I'm really sorry."

I climbed in the backseat and gazed out of the window until we pulled back up at the house, where I went straight to sleep, but not before throwing away every pattern and cloth that reminded me of that night.

CHAPTER 52
SIOBHAN

For the next two weeks, Carmen sulked and moped around the house, not really speaking to anyone and barely participated in school. I felt terrible for her, because I knew winning that fashion show meant everything to her. The only thing that would cheer her up was watching cartoons with Chase. Even then, she couldn't win, because Chase owned the remote whenever Rugrats came on.

On my way out of the house for the day, I laid out on the sofa beside her. She did a bad job of pretending not to know I was there. I waved my hand in front of her face and the corners of her mouth began to tremble.

Finally, she burst out laughing and pushed me away from her. "Where are you going all spiffed up? Another date with your *boyfriend*?" she asked, batting her eyes at me.

"Actually, don't tell Mama, but I have my first audition today."

"Audition? When were you planning to tell me? Have you rehearsed? Oh my God, Siobhan! I'm so proud of you!" she screamed.

"Shhh! Will you be quiet? I don't want anybody to know, just in case I don't get it," I whispered.

"Well, for one, you're walking into this whole thing with the wrong mindset. You have to own it, and know you deserve it. Where's your confidence, girl?"

I was still working on my self-confidence, but nothing would've made me more anxious than my mama knowing I was going after a career as an actress. She always preached to me about getting a job in a field where there would be no shortage of work, and that acting was a hobby, and nothing more.

"So, what's the role for? Do you get to kiss a hot guy? Wait, is that okay with Tremaine? Girl, you got issues!" she said, gushing all over me like it was her audition.

It was nice to see her smiling again. She loved digging into my life because for so long, it lacked any excitement. The thought of me becoming a famous actress make us both squeal.

"To answer your questions, it's a small role in a film about slavery. I would be working in the fields. I don't have to kiss anybody, and Tremaine is actually taking me," I replied.

"Well, good luck! One of us needs a win, big time!" When Tremaine knocked on the door, I grabbed Chase and we headed out. Tremaine tried to wave at Carmen as I closed the door in both their faces. I didn't want to be late, because I knew we needed time to find parking and time for me to settle my nerves before going inside.

"You ready?" he asked.

"I think so."

We pulled up to a small studio in East Hollywood and sat there while I hyperventilated.

"Relax," Tremaine said. "You can do this. Right little man?"

Chase clapped and mumbled a bunch of mixed up words, but I was catching what he was throwing. I planted a kiss on Tremaine's lips and got out. I kept replaying his and Carmen's last words to me as I sat in the waiting area. Over 100 girls showed up to try out for the same role and a few others. We all looked so different that it was hard to tell what they were looking for.

"Siobhan Butler?" a petite woman called out, sticking her head out of a door.

I stuffed my script in my purse and went for it. The room was empty except for two long tables where four people who looked nothing like me sat, glaring at me with the most serious faces. The woman who called me in the room turned on a video camera and said, "We're ready when you are".

I was a few lines into my audition when my mouth dried up and I started mispronouncing and slurring my words. I didn't even make it through to the last line when I was cut off.

"Thank you. We'll be in touch if we're interested," the lady said.

No one else in the room ever spoke to me. They just whispered back and forth in each other's ears. I couldn't tell if they liked me or not, so I tried not to panic, because the hard part was over. Whether they called back or not, I knew I gave it my all.

On my walk back to the car, I heard clapping and cheering. I looked up and it was Tremaine and Chase, holding a bouquet of roses. "Congratulations, baby girl. You did it!" Tremaine said.

"But we don't even know if I got the part," I said, as he pulled me close, while Chase climbed all over the hood of my car.

"It don't matter. Sometimes you win. Sometimes you lose. The thing to remember is you tried. And tomorrow, you're going to try again. That's how this thing is going to work, going forward. Okay?"

I can't say I wasn't turned on, but the feeling of someone finally believing in me was indescribable. "Okay," I replied, as we exchanged a cute peck on the lips.

Tremaine grabbed my arm as I turned to head back to the car. "One more thing," he said. He pulled a small box from his pocket and wiped the beads of sweat from his forehead. "I want you to know how special you are to me, and how no matter how hard things get between us, I got your back. This ring is my promise to you, that as long as you're not willing to give up on me, I won't give up on you. Oh, and I love you too."

With tears in my eyes, I accepted my promise ring and we hugged and kissed again. I smiled for the rest of the evening, so much that when I walked through the door at home, Carmen blocked the hallway. "Come on, let me lay him down first, and I'll tell you all about it," I told her. I came back to a freshly popped bag of popcorn and two cups of red Kool-aid.

"Okay, let's hear it," she said, smiling from ear to ear.

CHAPTER 53

TREMAINE

Getting ready for prom was a real out-of-body experience for me. I ended up rocking the last look from Carmen's line at the fashion show, and I borrowed a pair of Stacy Adams from Uncle Tony. But my fit wasn't complete until I spritzed my favorite Polo cologne around my neck. Before we left to go get the girls, Uncle Tony filled up two disposable cameras with pics of me from every angle.   He was still trying to fix my collar and tie when Carmen called.

"Where are you? We're gonna be late," she fussed.

"I'm coming, I'm coming. We'll be there in a minute."

She hung up before I could say another word, so I

grabbed my jacket, wallet and a pack of gum and hit the door.

They made us wait in the living room until the girls were ready. Her mom came out first and stood there, with her hands on her hips. "I know you didn't come in here without some flowers or something," she said.

"Oh, shoot," I said, as I ran back out to Unc's car to grab her corsage. When I came back in, Carmen was coming down the hallway. She had a thin, pink gown on that was covered in rhinestones, that covered her feet. Her hair was pulled up into a shiny but stiff bun, and she had clear chopsticks in her head. She held the sides of her dress and twirled, smiling.

"How do I look?" she asked.

"You aight," I said, laughing.

"Wait 'til you see your girl. We hooked her up."

I stood up as I heard her coming down the hallway, knocking into the walls. Her mom had her arms around her waist, helping hold her up, until she met me near the back of the couch.

"Wow," I said, as I took in every inch of her.

Ms. Shanté pulled some of her hair back into a small bun, and the braids that were hanging led to a beautiful, red gown that hung off of her shoulders, then stopped at her knees. I couldn't be mad at that split over her thighs. That dress draped over her figure just right.

"Turn around for me?" I asked.

She gave me the silliest look and pointed to her shoes. "Right," I said, as everybody laughed.

"You better get going," Ms. Shanté said.

We piled inside of Siobhan's car. I drove, of course, because Carmen and Siobhan were too busy worrying about the wind messing up their hair. By the time we got to the gym, the parking lot was packed. I helped both of them out of the car and we walked like three old people, trying to get to the door.

"Don't worry. I have a change of shoes in the car. I just need to make it through our pictures," Siobhan said.

As we turned over our tickets and got our hands stamped, my heart started racing. "Y'all ready?" I asked. They smiled at me, and we walked in, stopping at the entrance to take in all of the class of 2000 going crazy on the dance floor.

"I'm going to get us something to drink. I'll be right back," I said.

Siobhan kissed my cheek and Carmen helped her wobble over to a row of chairs that were lined up on a wall. I was fixing our drinks and minding my own business when Brandy walked up. "You look really nice tonight," she shouted, trying to drown out the loud music.

"Thanks!"

Surprisingly, she grabbed her drink and moved on. Her skin was so pale, she looked sick. Carmen met me halfway across the gym for her drink, as she headed to the dance floor. "What did Brandy want?" she shouted, pressing her face against my ear.

"She was being nice for a change."

"Oh?" she shouted. "Well, I'm gonna dance. Let me know when you guys are ready to go. Have fun!"

"You too," I shouted.

When I got back over to Siobhan, she was slouched over, with her legs open. Her shoes were sitting beside her, and she didn't look like she was having the slightest bit of fun. "Wanna dance?" I asked. She just took her drink and shook her head. "What's wrong?"

"Nothing. I'm just taking it all in," she said.

After sitting on the wall with her for a few minutes, I managed to convince her to go take our pictures. We even took a group picture with Carmen. She was too hype, throwing up fake gang signs and stuff. Then, when we got back out to the party, the DJ slowed the music down. "Computer Love" came on, and I pulled Siobhan to the dance floor, when she was headed back for her seat.

I pulled her closer, wrapping my hands around her waist, but she looked like she was in pain, so I bent down and unbuckled her shoes, helping her step out of them. We stared into each other's eyes, cheesing, until she laid on my shoulder and swayed her hips to the beat. We danced like that for the rest of the night, no matter what song came on.

After everybody started leaving, we found a diner and ordered just about everything we could fit in our stomachs before going back to Siobhan's house to crash. I slept on the floor beside her bed, holding her hand until my arm went numb. I think it was safe to say she had a good time. She didn't complain about her feet after our first dance, and anything she asked for, she got, until I closed my eyes for the night.

CHAPTER 54

SIOBHAN

When my alarm went off, I didn't instantly jump up. Carmen wore enough excitement for both of us. For me, it was a bittersweet day. I knew things were about to get real in my life, and I knew there was no way I was going to get through everything coming my way, without my friends. I closed my eyes and said a prayer before stepping foot out of bed. Before I could finish, the bed was shaking, and Carmen was screaming. "Get up! Wake up, Siobhan! It's graduation day!"

As soon as her feet hit the bed again, I grabbed her ankle and fell on her butt. We both laughed hysterically as she pulled herself up.

When I went to brush my teeth, the smell of bacon filled the house, making my stomach growl. Mama stuck her head in the bathroom and said, "Good morning, my baby! You ready for today?" She disappeared before I was able to answer. I couldn't help but to smile, as butterflies rolled around in my lower stomach. I was 18 years old, graduating high school, and she was still calling me her baby.

After breakfast, Mama got Chase dressed up in the cutest little suit and gave him two braids to the back with a tiny hat to match. She jumped fresh in a red jumper that flowed over her short, thick frame. Her makeup was banging, and she made the house smell amazing when she spritzed a cotton candy scented body spray all over herself.

I grabbed my white mini dress from the closet, pulled it down over my hips, and checked my booty in the mirror. "It's still there," Carmen said, laughing.

"Why aren't you dressed?" I asked.

She pulled a hot pink dress out with a pair of pink platform sandals to match. "You think she'll show up?" she asked.

"How could she not? She is still your mom. Give her another chance. If she shows up, just live in the moment…Oh, and that dress is poppin' by the way."

When we finished getting ready, we all piled into Mama's car. Things didn't start to feel real until I was in my seat, waiting for my row to go up and get our diplomas. I looked for Chase to blow him a kiss, and he was in Daddy's lap, with his new woman right beside him. Daddy shot me a thumbs up and I held my head up and strutted across the stage, took my picture, and waltzed back to my seat. My adrenaline was pumping, and I was high on life.

Back at the house, Mama had decked out the entire living room with graduation decorations. She bought a big ole cake for me, Carmen and Tremaine to share, all with our baby pictures on it. She fussed at Daddy as soon as his new girlfriend left. "Now, who's that one?" she asked, laughing. Daddy just shook his head and topped off his drink.

"Mind your business," he said, after a huge gulp.

Later, Tremaine and I sat outside on the porch for a while, watching the fireflies light up the night. He kissed my forehead and got up to run inside. When he returned with a big slice of cake, he fed me a few bites, before eating the rest. For the rest of the evening, we sang karaoke, overate, played board games, and passed out just before sunrise.

I woke up and everybody was gone, so I sat out on the porch and watched the cars go by, reflecting, laughing, and even crying a little. High school wasn't as bad as I expected. Keeping Chase a secret ended up working in my favor. I knew people had their thoughts about me and talked about me behind my back because none of them knew anything about my personal life until I started dating Tremaine. But when it came down to what really mattered, I was in a much better place that where I started a year ago. I was looking forward to the future and my new life that included a loving boyfriend and a new family and friends that I never knew I needed.

With Tremaine going off to college way across the country, I didn't know what the future held for us, but I still had my ring and honored his promise, until he told me otherwise.

CHAPTER 55

TREMAINE

The one good thing to come out of coming to stay with Uncle Tony was learning to tie a bow tie. I didn't know if it was my nerves or what, but I was about ready to give up and throw it out the window when Unc walked in, halfway dressed, smelling like a cologne ad from a magazine. "Come here," he said, grabbing the tie from the floor by the window, and fixing my shirt. He was really focused, to the point of sweating, trying to get the tie around my neck. When he finished, he stepped back and smiled like a proud father.

"You ready?" he asked. I turned and looked at myself in the mirror on my dresser and smiled. When I realized that

I had forgot to clean my golds, I grabbed my rag from my dresser and found a gift-wrapped box underneath.

As I opened it, so many thoughts crossed my mind. My granny always wanted to see me walk across the stage and get my diploma. My mama never had goals or aspirations for me because she didn't even come close to finishing, herself. I couldn't help but to think about the days where I needed help with my homework, and she would laugh and poke fun at me for trying. I sometimes wondered if she would've even shown up for me if she was still alive.

Unc left the room right when I was ready to open the box. In no time, he came back and said, "You have a call". When Travis's deep voice vibrated in my ear, I got a little choked up. I thought he was going to be able to make it, but his probation officer wouldn't approve travel out of the state.

"Congrats, Knucklehead. I always knew it was you who would prove Mama wrong. Granny probably all the way up there in heaven telling everybody about her baby," Travis said, laughing.

"'Preciate that," I said. "I wish you could've come. We need more time to catch up. Man, you would love Cali. It's beautiful here."

"I bet it is. But you know that ain't my style. Ain't nothing out there for a convict like myself. You oughta see folk's faces when they ask what I went to jail for, and I tell them. It's hard out here bro."

"Yeah, I get it. I was thinking about going to school out there anyway. You know Gram been on my radar since that time we went to the battle of the bands. It ain't the same without y'all, man."

"Well, look. I gotta go catch this bus to see a honey about some money. Then, tonight, I'm hittin' the rink and celebrating, in your honor. I love you, bro. For real. No matter what happens. I'm here for you, as soon as I get my shit together."

"I love you too, man. Everybody deserves a second chance. I got your back. Fa sho," I said.

"We need to leave," Unc said, as I hung up the phone. "You ready?"

I went back to my room and sat on the bed to finish opening my gift. My eyes burned and my throat was throbbing as I fought back the tears. It was a box of letters…from my granny. "I know you think I abandoned the family. Truth is, I had to get out of there. But I never stopped checking on y'all. I never stopped making sure y'all had as much as I could provide, and I never stopped loving my mama. I begged her to bring you and for y'all to come live with me a long time ago. She said she couldn't leave Travis down there by himself. But in almost every letter she wrote, she talked about all of these dreams she had for you and how she knew you were special. She wanted this and so much more for you. Thank you…for not letting her down."

I couldn't fight it anymore. "She said that? She said she thought I was special?" Unc grabbed and hugged me, with his fists in my back.

"I'm damn proud of you. I hope you don't take anything you've accomplished for granted. You have earned the right to be proud of yourself. You owe it to you, and you only, to go after everything you want," he said.

I couldn't bring myself to tell him I'd decided to go back home for college, to Grambling. Travis needed me and I needed him. I couldn't see Unc understanding our bond, because he wasn't close with my mama and he never had a brother. They were all I had, and I wanted to give Trav what Unc gave me…somebody to lean on.

The whole ride over to the stadium, my stomach just turned. When I finally put on my cap and gown in the parking lot and looked in the passenger side mirror, all of my breakfast came up. My stomach still didn't ease up and relief was nowhere in sight as I went to line up and saw Siobhan turn around at the front of the line. She had this glow, like the sun was reflecting off of her skin. It was like she had no idea how beautiful she was to me. I just watched as she talked, laughed and smiled with all of the people around her. When she finally looked at me, it was as if everything was alright in the world. Nothing else mattered. She waved and gave me a huge smile, blowing kisses over people's heads. She knew it made me uncomfortable to be emotional in public, but she didn't care. She was happy. I was happy. And we deserved every bit of it.

Then, it dawned on me that I hadn't seen Carmen. I should've passed her on the way to my spot. I looked back and there she was, nervously fixing that red lipstick in her little pocket mirror. When our eyes met, she smiled at me too. I'd never seen Carmen smile so big, considering the fact that she was graduating from high school and not a single family member was there to support her. This was a huge step for all of us, but we knew the real test would begin after that day, and we knew we would need each other for the rest of our lives.

The line finally started moving and we could hear the music and cheering from under the bleachers. Beyond walking across the stage and receiving my diploma, everything else was a blur. My mind ran crazy with all the possibilities of what I could become in my lifetime and suddenly, I was more excited than nervous.

After graduation, we went back to Siobhan's house for a small party. It was our usual crew, but we made the most of it. We ate and laughed all night. When no one was looking, I would hurry and wipe tears from my eyes before they had a chance to fall. I had never known what it really felt like to be happy. I had real friends, a girl I loved and a promising career in computer technology. If you had asked me two years ago where I wanted to go in life, I wouldn't have had an answer for you, because I never saw past a life in the streets. Living with Uncle Tony showed me a new way of thinking and introduced me to a life of possibilities.

When we couldn't keep our eyes open anymore, we all fell asleep wherever we were. I woke up on the floor of their living room. Siobhan was on the couch. Carmen was on the floor beside me. Pop cans, half eaten slices of cake and empty pizza boxes were all over the place. Since I was the first to wake up, aside from little Chase, I started cleaning. The house phone rang while I was emptying the trash. After three rings, and nobody budged, I finally answered. "Come home," Unc said. His voice sounded unusually raspy, like he was still in bed.

When I headed back to the living room, Carmen was lying there, eyes wide open, looking at the ceiling. "You feel any different?" she asked. I fumbled my words, trying to answer her in a way that made sense. I didn't really feel any different, but I knew that if I had any hope of getting home in a reasonable amount of time after Unc's call, it was then or never.

"Nah, I don't, but I have to go. Tell Siobhan I said I'll call her later."

After a long, deep breath, she closed her eyes and refocused on the ceiling. I almost busted my ass a couple of times running, dodging kids on the sidewalks on big wheels. I forgot Unc had scheduled a surprise for me for the morning after graduation. I was hoping I would've had time to slip in the house and change before he noticed, but he was sitting at the dining room table when I came in, sweating and out of breath. "Give me ten minutes," I said, clutching my chest. He just looked at me, with these swollen, puffy eyes, and his presence felt cold.

"Come sit down. I need to talk to you," he finally said.

"Nah, I'll stand. I don't want to be late. What's up? What's going on?"

When he dropped his head, my heart began to pound, and a chill went down my spine. Then, the phone rang. "I got it," I stuttered.

"Tremaine, come sit down," he demanded.

We let the phone ring until it went to voicemail.

"Unc, what's going on? You good?"

Suddenly, a woman's voice played on the answering machine.

"Hi, this message is for Antonio Johnson. This is Mae

Jenkins with Heavenly Gates Funeral Home. I saw we had a message from you regarding the receiving of the body of a Mr. Travis Johnson. Please call me back when you get this. We'd love to help you during this time and we're praying for you and your loved ones. The number is 318-222…"

Before I knew it, I had lost it. I slung the phone and answering machine across the room. "Nah, man! Nah! Don't tell me that. Come on, man. Unc! For real?" I cried, right before my fist went through the wall by the front door. I had felt pain in my life, but that was a different kind of pain. My best friend was gone. And the worst part? I wasn't there to protect him. He always promised me he wouldn't let anything bad happen to me. I was so mad that I couldn't give him the same in return.

My eyes and my face burned as tears poured. I couldn't see anything. I couldn't hear anything. I couldn't feel anything but pain of each breath I took before I dropped to my knees.

When I woke up a couple of hours later, I could hear Uncle Tony on the phone. My head was spinning like I'd fallen in a dream and couldn't catch myself. I was a mess. I stood by the couch, far away from Uncle Tony as he wrapped up his conversation. "Sit down," he said, trying to clear the lump in his throat.

"I feel like I'm in a bad dream, and I can't wake up," I said. Then, the tears started again.

"I know you're hurting. Whether you realize it or not, so am I. We already didn't have much family left as it was. Damn, this one hurts," Unc said.

"What...what happened?"

I knew I wasn't ready to hear it, but I just needed to know if he kept his word.

"He was out with some guys from the neighborhood. There was a concert at the skating rink. A fight broke out, and he asked a dude to take him home. They stopped at the corner store for something and whomever was fighting at the concert, met up at the corner store to fight. Cars were everywhere when the fight broke out. Then, somebody started shooting. The car he was in was blocked in, and a few bullets flew through the windshield and one pierced his heart. He was gone before they could get him to the hospital."

My body trembled as anger rushed through my veins and turned to sadness. It was the weakest I'd ever felt. I buried my face in my hands and fell apart again. We both did.

By the next weekend, I was back in a place that felt unfamiliar to me. It didn't feel like home anymore. We didn't even have the money to give him a proper funeral. But none of his boys showed up to the wake. Not even the chicken heads that always hustled him out of the money I sent him.

Me, Uncle Tony and Ms. Nadine were the only ones that showed up, and we prayed over his body before they lowered him into the ground. It was a little late for prayer, but it was the only thing that felt right.

Every time I think about that day, my heart aches, because I know he was just in the wrong place at the wrong time. Now he's gone. I had to live with not being there for him for the rest of my life. I should've stood up to Unc when Travis asked for a bus ticket out here for my graduation. I should've said something. Now that it's too late, all I can do is make the most of this life.

Losing the person that I loved the most in the world made everything else seem so small and unimportant, like me and Unc going back and forth over where I was going to school. I had no reason to go back to Louisiana, and once we got back home, my acceptance letter to USC was in the mail. Here I was getting a chance at a new life, at a great school with a chance to prepare for a great career, and I couldn't help but to think about if I would've been in that car too, had we never lost mama and granny.

CHAPTER 56

CARMEN

If you had told me a year prior that I'd be graduating from high school with two best friends and a promising future in fashion, I would've laughed in your face. From the ups and downs of trying to get Mami to grow up, to having to live with the Butlers, I didn't think I was going to make it to that day. As I stood in line, waiting to walk into the stadium, I couldn't help but laugh. I mean, I laughed uncontrollably, until a teacher walked up.

"Are you okay?" she asked.

I was bent over with pain in my side and tears in my

300

eyes, as everyone around me started laughing too. The teachers must've thought we were all crazy to have been laughing at absolutely nothing. Without smudging my mascara, I blotted my eyes as the line began to move.

The sounds of all of the girl's heels clanging on the concrete, under the bleachers, instantly became a mere whisper as all of our families screamed, whistled and chanted our names. The flash of cameras in the crowd made me feel like a superstar, as I imagined myself following a line of models out onto the catwalk at the end of my first show in New York Fashion Week.

The graduation theme music looped as our class of about 215 seniors walked across the football field. Girls were getting stuck in the grass, some even falling and exposing their parts unknown. The guys laughed instead of helping them up, and it still wasn't enough to keep everybody from cheering for us.

I scanned the crowd and locked eyes with Ms. Shanté. She smiled proudly as I found my seat. Her lack of response when I mouthed, "Mami?" let me know she wasn't there. When the ceremony began, I imagined her dying in a hospital or somewhere stuck in a car accident. I knew that there was no way she would miss my graduation unless there was a life and death situation.

Halfway through our valedictorian's speech and the sun melting my thighs, I noticed a man watching me from the crowd. I covered my legs and tried to look away, but I could still feel him staring me down. Luckily, the presentation of the diplomas came, and I had something to distract me. I waited my turn at the stairs and again stared into the crowd. The sun nearly blinded me as I searched for her one last time. Then, from the third row, I heard Siobhan call out, "Hold your head up!"

When my name was called, I stepped up on that stage, corrected my posture and crossed with my head in the air. As soon as my diploma was in my hand, I blew Siobhan a kiss. She caught it and held it close to her heart and smiled as I stepped down.

The time finally came for us to switch our tassels to the other side of our caps. I watched as everybody else lit up and followed the principal's instructions and tossed their caps into the sky. I kept mine and pulled out a letter I had wrote to myself when I moved in with the Butlers.

I sat back down to read it as the space around me cleared out. I couldn't bring myself to finish it as the first sentence became obscured by the running ink, re-activated by my tears. When a tissue blocked the bottom half of my letter, I felt Siobhan and Ms. Shanté wrap their arms around me. Siobhan took the letter from my hands and read it out loud.

"Dear Carmen,

The next phase of your life is going to be scary. It's going to feel like you're alone at times, and you may be, but when things get tough, you'll always have your new family to lean on. They're pretty great too. And when you graduate college in four years, they're going to be right there, cheering for you beside Mami and Papi, hopefully.

You're going to go on to become a world-renowned fashion designer and take over the world, one expensive fabric at a time. Cleaning toilets will be a thing of the past, and you will be doing the hiring. People will come to you for answers and you won't have all of them, but you will be able to afford to put someone on payroll to have them handle those questions for you.

Cry if you must. Fall down if you must. But giving up on your dreams is never an option, under any circumstances. Like Mami always says, "Suck it up and figure it out". You will survive high school and one day, you will be unstoppable. Be brave. Be strong. And most of all, be you, Carmen Valentina Martinez."

When she was done, I felt stronger than ever…like a new woman. It's funny how so much could change in just four years. Some would say I was young and gullible to believe I could be everything I ever dreamt of and more. But I was well on my way, and as long as I have my friends, I know I'll be fine.

On the way back to the car, the man from earlier was standing near the exit with a beautiful bouquet of roses. His greasy hair and tired, hazel eyes told the story of a man who had been through a lot.

Before he could step forward, Mami stepped out from behind him with the biggest smile on her face. I looked around to see if everyone else was as shocked as I was. Ms. Shanté just smiled and encouraged me to embrace the moment with a soft nudge.

"Did you seriously think I would miss this day?" Mami asked.

My face probably said, "Um, yeah", but my heart was ready to burst into a million pieces at any moment. I just ran into her arms and stayed there for as long as I could. She stroked my hair like she used to when I was little and kissed my forehead. Then, she pulled away from me, cleaning her face.

"Say hi!" she said.

"I'm sorry. Are you a new boyfriend, or…?"

He extended his hands and placed the bouquet in my arms and pulled me close. "Mija, I've waited 18 years for this day," he said.

"Papi? Mami, how did you…you did this?" I shouted, leaping into his arms.

"Hi, Carmen. I'm Ernesto Gutierrez. I'm your father, and it's a pleasure to finally meet you," he said.

"I'm so happy to finally meet you. Is it okay if I ride with you back to Ms. Shanté's house? She's throwing us a party."

Mami and Papi had these strange looks on their faces as they cleared a path to the exit. My head was pounding has it overflowed with all of the *what-ifs* and *maybes*. When I finally managed to pull my head out of the clouds, just a few short feet from a white car, a guy with the same greasy hair as Papi, rocking a black and white checkered blazer with a pair of ocean blue dress pants stood near the trunk with his head hanging low. "We have a driver too?" I asked as I trotted happily to the backseat.

After clearing my throat a time or two, Mami and Papi's faces changed again.

"Carmen, we have something to tell you," Mami said.

"This is your older brother, Alejandro," Papi said, halfway trying to smile.

The distance between him and Mami grew immediately, as my armpits began to itch.

"So, you mean to tell me, not only did you keep my father away from me my entire life, I had a brother who you just up and abandoned, just like you did me? What else have you been lying about? Were you ever really abused?" I shouted.

Papi and Alejandro walked to the front of the car as Papi gave Mami the nastiest look. She was on her own and it was clear that she had been lying about a lot more than being abused.

"Mija, just listen," she said.

"No, I'm done listening to you. You are a damn liar! How do you sleep at night knowing you've ruined three lives? What did I do to deserve a mother like you? This has to be the worst day of my life!"

I ripped my heels off and started down the driveway toward the street. The Butlers pulled up beside me and stopped. "Get in," Siobhan said. I looked back and Mami and Papi were at each other's throats. Alejandro sat in the backseat with his head still hanging low.

The best part about the party was celebrating my official first day of freedom from Mami. Over the last few years, she everything I used to love about her disappeared. Things weren't just perfect before, but she always found a way to make up for it in other ways. At some point, she just stopped caring, and over time, I stopped caring about wanting to know why.

I didn't win the scholarship from the fashion show, but I learned a lot in the process. I learned that in life, I won't win at everything. Sometimes I will fail, but to get to where I was trying to go, I would have to get back up.

It broke my heart to watch Brandy take home that prize that I had worked so hard for. But losing it just taught me that I would always need a backup plan for when things didn't go my way. I would have never expected to hear that the scholarship prize had been revoked from Brandy because she was no longer going to college. She later came by and asked to talk, then let me know she was expecting, and had no plans of getting an abortion, so it was only right that she gave me what I deserved. She said that the school didn't normally give away the scholarship after it had been revoked, but she managed to write a pretty detailed letter explaining why I deserved it, and they agreed.

I'm kind of grateful that things worked out the way that they did, because had I won, I would have flown across the country to go to school in New York. But what kind of life would that have been without the people I love the most not being there by my side when I needed them?

I spent that night with Siobhan and Tremaine thinking about how nothing would ever be the same for me after that day. I was in control of my own life and it felt pretty good and pretty scary at the same time. I didn't sleep much at all that night, but I did pretend to be asleep when Tremaine woke up and started cleaning. He was about to slip out of the door when I caught him looking at me crazy from the corner of my eye.

Later the next day, I met up with Papi and Alejandro to spend time getting to know each other. I had to admit that after all of those years of longing for that relationship, it didn't feel how I thought it would. Papi and I just didn't click. Alejandro was quiet and didn't speak an ounce of English, and I was just feeling awkward the whole time.

Mami didn't come around at all that day. She knew I wasn't feeling her, and there was nothing she could do or say to change that.

By sunset, some guy was picking them up in a van, and that was the last time I saw or spoke to either of them. Although it didn't go the way I had dreamt it would, I was happy to have that hole in my heart repaired. Nothing I had hoped and prayed for worked out for me during my last year of high school, but to say it was a total bust would've been a lie. I got everything I never knew I wanted or needed.

I found a new family with the Butlers, I got my scholarship after all, and I gained a sister and best friend. Tremaine's okay too. Had it not been for Ms. Shanté taking us in, I don't know where I would have ended up, but the past was behind me, and I was ready to conquer the world, one poorly dressed person at a time.

two months later

CHAPTER 57

SIOBHAN

It was a struggle getting things back to normal when
Tremaine came back from Louisiana. He didn't tell us about
his brother until he called to ask for a ride home from the
airport. I could see the pain in his eyes, and I wanted to be
there for him, but he had grown distant.

When he got home, we didn't talk for a long time. I
occupied my mind with everything under the sun. From
looking for a job, to helping Carmen look for an apartment, I
made sure I wasn't just sitting on my hands. I dropped by one
day and left him a card in the door and moved on. I knew

how much he loved his brother, and how much he had been looking forward to moving back home to be closer to him.

I must say, the idea of him not leaving for college made me pretty happy, but I was forced to bury my excitement when he finally called. I had never gotten dressed that fast before in my life. Chase and Mama were out seeing some of her friends, and Carmen and I hopped in the car and headed over. I nearly knocked him down when he opened the door. He squeezed me so tight that he picked me up off the floor and swung me around. I loaded him down with kisses and didn't care that Uncle Tony had come out of his room and stood there while I geeked out. When I stepped back and gave him a once over, I fought back the tears so hard. Carmen brushed past me and buried her face in his chest.

He was the one who lost his brother, and we were the ones standing there, crying like some fools. When Carmen was done, I went back in. "I missed you so much," I mumbled, and he kissed my forehead as we rocked from side to side.

"I missed you more," he said.

The elephant in the room sat down on the couch and flipped on the tv. Tremaine nodded for me to go over and speak. Of course, I pouted, but he insisted.

I sat beside Uncle Tony and pretended to be interested in what he was watching. "Hey," I said. How've you been?"

"I'm okay. How are you?" he asked.

"I'm better now," I said, looking over my shoulder at Tremaine, smiling.

He and Carmen were laughing and talking while Uncle Tony and I struggled.

"He talked about you the whole time we were gone. We're all he's got now, so if you plan to stick around, please treat him right," Uncle Tony said.

"I plan to," I replied.

He grabbed me around my neck and pulled me in for a hug. "I thought you hated me," I said.

He looked at me and laughed. "I never hated you. I don't hate anybody. I just wanted him to focus, that's all. I thought I knew what was best for him."

"Thank you," I said.

He looked at me strangely.

"For what?"

"Everything. Had you never taken him in, we never would've met. Whether you realize it or not, he loves and looks up to you. As hard as your rules have been to follow, for him, he respected them and you."

I nearly jumped out of my skin when Carmen grabbed me from behind. "Come on. Let's go get food! You want something, Unc?" she asked.

"I'm good. Y'all go on," he replied.

While we were out grabbing food, we rode by the apartments Carmen had applied for. While she was inside checking on her application, Tremaine turned to me with this goofy grin. "So, what you thinking? he asked.

"About?"

"Your mom said you gotta go, right? Uncle Tony gave me my walking papers before graduation. So, you wanna go half on an apartment with me?"[1]

"Wait, apartment? I thought you were going back to Louisiana…"

"My life is here now. Louisiana will always be home, but I think I should stay here for a while," he said.

The thought had never crossed my mind, and quite honestly, I became so overwhelmed at the thought of living with him, that I didn't immediately respond. Luckily, Carmen came dancing down the sidewalk. "I got the apartment!" she shouted.

I was so happy for her. Before we even got back to the house, she was talking about all of the different ways she envisioned decorating her first place. "I'm kind of glad you're not going to New York," I told her.

"I love you! You can't get rid of me that easily."

When we dropped Tremaine off, he gave me a long

kiss and said, "Think about it".

As soon as he closed the door, Carmen climbed in the front seat and asked, "Think about what?"

"He asked me about getting a place together. I'm not sure if I'm ready," I said.

"At this point, your mom has made it clear. You don't have a choice, and you can't afford to live on your own."

I hated to admit it, but she was right. Since I opted out of college, for the time being, I had to get a job, or two.

Later on that night, when I asked Mama about possibly moving in with Tremaine, she left me confused. It was more of what she didn't say that worried me. Her body language said, "Girl don't do it," but her mouth said, "Sounds good to me."

We looked for apartments during his days off and in between my job interviews. Finally, we found the perfect one, but I had to show proof of employment and nobody would hire me for the jobs I was applying for, with no experience. Mama broke down and hired me to work with her after she picked up two more clients. I later landed a second job as a waitress at a night club.

It was important that Tremaine and I made our schedules work so that we didn't have the added expense of paying for daycare for Chase. I would come home from working at the club, catch a quick nap, then be up with Chase when Tremaine would wake him up with his music as he got ready for class. Now and then, Carmen and Mama would sometimes help us with him whenever our schedules clashed. I was looking forward to the fall when Chase would start pre-school. With his fourth birthday coming up, it was a huge relief to know he would be in school most of the day while we worked.

I was getting bookings left and right when I started networking with my customers at night. Tremaine was supportive and surprisingly, we got along great. I couldn't have been happier with the way things fell into place for us.

CHAPTER 58

CARMEN

It wasn't much, but it was mine. I'd never lived on my own before, and my first apartment was a studio. With the money I'd saved, I managed to grab me a bed from a yard sale, a small sofa from the Butler's babysitter and a colored tv and stand from Tremaine's family's pawn shop. A few personal touches finally made it feel like home. An area rug and antique coffee table filled the space between my bed and tv and a tv dinner tray sat just under my sofa for me to enjoy my meals on.

It was quiet. A quiet I'd never really experienced before. Nobody was asking me to do anything, go anywhere or change my clothes because they had company coming over.

I think I cried in the shower the first few nights, as the hot water massaged my neck and back. In the first week of being in my new place, my phone never rang. I specifically asked to be left alone during that time, so that I could think and plan my next steps carefully.

After talking to Ms. Shanté, I understood that I could be on my own and be successful, right here in LA. Besides, New York was way more expensive, and I was afraid to admit that while I wanted to live alone, I didn't want to be completely alone. It was hard for me to make friends, and I had found some pretty amazing ones right here at home.

My first visitor banged on my door so hard, I thought it was the police. I'd barely cracked the door open when Siobhan fell into my arms. Chase latched on to my leg and Tremaine breezed past our girly moment to have a look around. "Nice place you got here," he said. "How does it feel…Being an adult and all?"

"It feels pretty damn good. To what do I owe this visit?"

"We both had the day off and wanted to see if you wanted to spend a day at the beach with us. Just a little fun and sun! So, how about it?" Siobhan asked.

"I wish I could, but I have somewhere to be in about

317

an hour. I actually should be getting ready to head out to catch my cab here in a few."

"Oh, care to share? You wouldn't happen to be going to your new job as an assistant to the tightest designer and stylist on the west coast, would you?" Siobhan asked, clearly more excited than I was.

"I agreed to meet Mami at a diner for lunch and to talk."

"Oh. You ready for that? I know how mad you were about her lying to you," Siobhan said.

"That's actually what she wanted to talk about. I don't know. I'm not getting my hopes up. That was a pretty big lie. I didn't see how she could explain keeping my brother from me my whole life. She had no idea how alone I felt all those times she was gone. "We'll see," I said.

"Let us drop you off," Tremaine said. "You don't need to be getting in cars with strangers."

I grabbed my bag and sun hat from the counter and took him up on the offer. When I arrived at the diner, Mami wasn't there yet. I sat in a small booth near a window where I could watch people as they walked by. I styled them in my head and laughed at their terrible choices in matching patterns and new blouses with out of style trousers. Mami walked by, rocking a hot orange sundress, with a sleek bun pulled to the back. She was always cute, thanks to me.

I waved as she looked around for me.

"Mija! You look so good!" She said, kissing me all over my face.

I sat across from her as she picked up a menu and covered her face.

"So, you wanted to talk to me?" I asked.

"Geez, baby. Let me order first. We have time, right?"

A few minutes into our meal, she was constantly calling our waitress over, asking for extra silverware and complaining about food she was almost done eating.

"Mami, what did you need to talk to me about?" I asked, as she took a bite.

"Okay. I know you're probably still mad at me about not telling you about your brother," she said, trying to sound concerned but her face told a different story.

"You think that was all I was mad about? Mami, you lied to me, my entire life! You told me that Papi was abusive, that he hurt you all the time. That's why you left. Why would you lie about something like that?" I shouted, as the other people in the restaurant turned and looked at me. "What?" I shouted.

"Lower your voice. Okay, the plan was for me to come to America first, find a job and a place to live, then Papi, and Alejandro were supposed to come later," she said.

"So, what changed? How could you just leave them behind like that?" I cried.

"Carmen, moving to a new country, without doing things the proper way, was hard for me. I was here all alone…scared out of my mind. I was pregnant with you and it took me a long time to find work. When I did, they fired me after they learned I was using someone else's ID and social security number."

"Where was Papi?"

"Mija, this is going to be hard for you to hear…but your father was in deep with a lot of bad people back home. He owed people money… lots of it. On top of that, we were in hiding because so many people wanted him dead. He found a friend who knew a way into America, but the guy could only take one of us. Papi didn't want to leave any of us behind," she said, beginning to sniffle.

"Why lie to me about who he was? You made me hate him for hurting you, and this whole time, it was you who hurt him!"

"That's not how it happened and that was never my intention," she lied.

"I can't believe you. You've had so many chances to bring them here, and you didn't, because you were too busy chasing other men. Did Papi know about Elisio? Did he know about any of the stuff you were doing? You know what? I'm done listening to your lies. I can't trust anything you say anymore.

The waitress laid the receipt on our table just in time. I sat the money for the bill on top of it and left. While I was outside calling for a ride, Mami came out behind me.

"Please, leave me alone," I yelled.

"I'm still your mother. You will respect me. You will not yell at me again. Everything I did for you was out of love. No, I did not make the best decisions all the time, but I tried. I gave you so much that I never had. Not once did you ever say, "Thank you". One day you will have kids. You will see. I did what I had to because I love you.

"I'm never having kids if there's any chance they'll turn out like you. Don't call me again," I said, as my cab driver pulled up.

I was done feeling sorry for her, tired of crying, and done letting people bring me down. From that day on, I decided to put the past behind me and look forward to my new life.

On my first day of work, it was hard adjusting to catering to someone else's vision. I wanted so badly to be giving all of my time and attention to my work. In my spare time, I did just that. I had started making new friends in school and it was nice to have people in my space who understood my way of thinking.

I didn't hear from Mami again, until Ms. Shanté came

by one day. She sat in the car looking like a lost puppy as Ms. Shanté and I talked at my front door. "She needs you," she said. "You need each other."

I looked over her shoulder as Mami looked straight ahead with a bag on her lap.

"I can only give her a few months, then she has to go," I responded.

"I can't ask you for more than that. Just promise me one thing," Ms. Shanté said. "Let up some. She's been through a lot. I know you have too. Just try to be there for each other. You only get one mom. Enjoy it while you can."

Ms. Shanté gave me a long, comforting hug, leaving a kiss print from her red lipstick on my cheek. I followed her to her car to help Mami with her bags. Once she was settled, Mami handed me an envelope.

"I got a new job at that diner we ate at a few weeks ago. It's not everything I owe you, but I can get you the rest in a week or so," Mami said. "I'm sorry...About everything. No more lies, I promise."

"I love you," I said.

"I love you too," Mami replied.

CHAPTER 59

TREMAINE

After we laid Travis to rest, I pretty much just shut down. My soul was numb, and I couldn't think about nothin' but him every day. From the time I woke up, to the time I went to sleep, I could see his face. I could still hear his corny ass laugh whenever we talked about Unc. Nobody ever knew how much it hurt him to not be able to bury Mama and Granny. People started treating him like some kind of animal. But he was just a kid.

Uncle Tony stepped up for me when I needed him the most, but I wish he would've been around more, and sooner, because Trav needed him too.

When me and Siobhan moved into our place, I hung the only picture I had of me and Travis and sat it on the table beside my bed. Seeing his 10-year-old face every day, smiling without a care in the world, gave me something to look forward to. I still had time to do all the things we used to talk about. What I didn't plan for was having somebody as dope as Siobhan by my side through it all. She really was perfect for me.

Since getting into our first apartment, getting new jobs and getting ready to start school had taken over our lives, I decided to plan a trip for us. Carmen was hesitant at first about leaving, but when I mentioned New York, she lost her mind. "When do we leave?" she asked.

"I actually thought we could drive out there and catch a flight back. Y'all down?" I asked.

"You know I'm down, Siobhan said, hopping into my lap and squeezing my neck. "This is gonna be so much fun!"

"New York, huh?" Carmen asked, beginning to tear up. "I don't even know what to say."

"Just say you're down to ride," I told her.

She stood up in the middle of the living room, twiddling her thumbs, then started jumping up and down, screaming and dancing, "I'm going to New York! I'm going to New York!"

Unc and Ms. Shanté finally stopped playing around

and got together. He even moved in with her. Whitney's mom was a thing of the past. And since things were going so good with me and Siobhan, they volunteered to rent us a brand-new white Mustang GT for our road trip.

When it was time for us to go, Siobhan obsessed over making sure Chase had everything he needed to stay behind with her mom. "Just give her your key," I said. She was so excited that she couldn't even get the key off the ring. Carmen had let the top down and was in the backseat standing up with the music thumping, dancing, while I loaded the trunk.

We had all kinds of chips, cookies, pops, and candy to keep us up during the drive. Ms. Shanté made us some sandwiches and boiled some eggs, that Siobhan was only able to eat with the top down, and she gave all of us a few extra dollars of spending money. Uncle Tony just stood to the side, with Chase on his back, watching our every move. We couldn't tell if he was excited or not, but he was definitely feeling some kind of way about us leaving.

When I closed the trunk, he walked up to me and reached for a hug. With his face pressed against my neck, he mumbled, "Have fun...and be safe. I love you". He stood back, sniffling and wiping his nose as Ms. Shanté joined him at the curb to watch us pull off. We could hear Chase's little voice shouting, "Bye, Mommy!" when we got to the end of the street. She turned around and waved at him until I turned the corner.

When I hit the on-ramp to I-10, I took off. My nerves began to settle as we got further away from LA. Siobhan held my hand and sang into the wind while Carmen had calmed down and took in the scenery along the sides of the highway. "We comin' back," I said, laughing.

"I know, boy. I just never thought I would ever get to see the rest of the country. We really graduated high school, y'all. We made it."

"We did," Siobhan said, turning to face Carmen. "I couldn't have done it without y'all. For real."

We were on our way to experiencing the trip of a lifetime and I could honestly say, I never expected my best friends to be a couple of bratty ass girls, but I wouldn't dare trade them for nothing in this world.

THE END

PLEASE LEAVE A REVIEW

If you liked this read and would recommend it to the teen or young adult fiction lover in your life, please leave a review on good reads and/or amazon.com. Please also tag us on Instagram to your posts when you receive your copy. Your support is greatly appreciated!

Instagram: exit81_publishing

COMING SOON...

(Young Adult -ages 14+)

Childhood friends, Trisha (Juicy), Nina and Michaela begin to question the future of their friendship when a catfish pits Michaela and Nina against one another as they try desperately to win his heart and secure a date for the Valentine's Day formal, hoping to turn in their nerd cards at school. Meanwhile, Juicy's new secret love forces her out of her comfort zone and into a world of trouble with her hip-hop legend of a mother. Sometimes friendships are meant to last forever, but how do you know it's real?

Add it to your Good Reads TBR today and sign up for our newsletter at www.exit81publishing.com to receive updates this release, giveaways and more.

ABOUT THE AUTHOR

Jakayla Gabrielle is an author from the Shreveport, Louisiana, with a love of storytelling for all ages. After discovering her passion for writing, while studying at Grambling State University, Jakayla set out on a mission to write relatable, page-turning books, that she hopes will inspire or encourage those who decide to indulge, to keep reading and follow their dreams.

www.ingramcontent.com/pod-product-compliance
Lightning Source LLC
Chambersburg PA
CBHW020246200626
46816CB00001BA/151